BLOODSHED IN CAMPUS

'Dipo Toby Alakija

ISBN: 978-07350-3-8
ISBN: 978-978-0735-0-3-6

Printed in United States
Published by the publishing house of

CALVARY ROCK RESOURCES

19, Ajina Street, Ikenne Remo,
Ogun State,
Nigeria.

36, Thomson road
Gorton
Manchester
M18 7QQ
United Kingdom

270 Madison Avenue
Suite 1500, New York, NY 10016
United States

www.calvaryrock.org

Dedication

This book is dedicated to thousands of innocent students who lost their lives in the crossfire, caused by conflicts between secret cults in many campuses in Nigeria, especially during the military regime.

ACKNOWLEDGMENTS

I must first acknowledge the encouragement I got from the Ogun State Ministry of Education, Science And Technology who, after going through the drama book that was first published in 2010, recommended that the book should be distributed in secondary schools, making it possible for Calvary Rock Resources Team to hold seminars that would curb the vice rings within the State in Nigeria.

I acknowledge the efforts of my ever adorable wife, Omolade Martha Alakija who is eager to get the results of my research work on social vices in this book to readers all over the world.

I really appreciate Adekunle Matthew Abiodun, the Director of Calvary Rock Resources for combining so many jobs together just to get things done. He and his team members like Tayo Akarigbo, Muyiwa Femi Alakija, Happy Benedict, Taiwo Peter (who provided secretarial services) and others are appreciated for their inputs.

My team of resource persons like Juwon Sokoya, Babalola Johnson, Roy Agboola, Lekan Somule and Jonathan Ayeri who helped me to source for materials for this book are appreciated.

My daughter, Toluwanimi Margaret Alakija, the Editor at Calvary Rock Resources is acknowledged and appreciated for taking time to critically study the book.

I must also acknowledge the contributions of Bankola Ola-Olukoyi, a lecturer at the Faculty of Arts at Olabisi Onabanjo University (formerly called Ogun State University) who turned the story into a screenplay. He complemented the results of my research works on social vices (which mostly focus on secret cults in Nigerian campuses) with materials that are within the confines of academic environment before turning the story into a movie for academic project in the University.

At this point, I must take the opportunity to say that this novel is full of materials that are based on factual events which took place at different locations, involving different people at different times. I wish to also add that now is the age when literary and research works must point out vices and their repercussions in our world. The issue especially about various faceless vice rings is so complex that nobody can claim to be an authority. It is becoming more complicated as more of dreadful vice rings get organized, growing into cancerous monsters that threaten the peace of the entire world

Going by the results of our research works on vice rings with Nigerian case studies, the institutions that are supposed to groom future leaders are turning into crime scenes. This non-fictional novel is a serious attempt to answer some basic questions like: what gives these vice rings so much power? What makes youths especially get involved in terrorism that turns innocent people victims of occult bloodshed and brutalities? In the cause of this research, so many people outside the campuses are involved or implicated. Many of them are politicians, academicians, godfathers and a host of others. This issue, however, is not really about them but about individuals, families, communities, the affected nations and the entire world.

CHAPTER ONE

Titi Moore rolled restlessly on the bed with her head full of different thoughts. It was well past mid night now, about three hours since she said to her children, "good night" and yet she was far from catching any night sleep. She found herself thinking of how she began her forty-five year old life up to the time she became a widow who had to cater for her three children with one of them already going to the University in a town that is about sixty kilometers away. Actually she would have loved Richard, her son who was admitted into the University to run his program on part time, but his uncle, Jibola, who was the only member of the extended family that was rich enough to give her a helping hand advised that Richard could study civil engineering on full time. Since Jibola was technically footing the bill of his academics, she had no choice but to go along with his decision. Her main concern was that Richard might be influenced to join the secret cults which were becoming more and more rampant in all the tertiary institutions in the country. She had heard stories about how many students have become victims of the vice rings. Hundreds, if not thousands of students, mostly innocent ones have lost their lives through the operations of secret cults. She could not quite understand why the government found it difficult to curb the vice ring that was growing out of hands in virtually all the campuses within the country.

She was afraid really but she knew she needed to talk to her son and make him realize what she had been through while trying to cater for him and other children in the hostile environment. She was almost sure he would listen and relieve her of her anxiety if she poured out her concern to him. The good thing about all her children was that they were obedient to her, not only because they appreciated the value she had added to their lives but were also sympathetic of the fact that she had to resist so many temptations when they lost their father in a ghastly motor accident. She noticed their affections and commitments to her while telling them how her life began.

Titi was the last child in the family of six. There were six children but two died consecutively at infant ages. When Titi was born, her parents did all they could to make live, including going to the witch doctors who told them to pamper the child, giving her everything she needed. She was spoilt rotten. She would get virtual everything she wanted by merely pointing at it. She has everything her parents could afford except education, ranging from clothes, choice food, toys and the like. However, she was not as educated as her two sisters and brother because she did not want to go to school. Her parents tried to let her see the need for education but she was too young to appreciate why she has to attend school where children of ages were scolded. Even when she attempted attending a primary school back in those days, she realized it was a completely different from the environment she was used to. Unlike when she was at home where she was almost worshiped, the teacher would order everybody to work and give them rules to follow as if they were adults. Failure to obey them would call for the strokes of the cane, saying they were act of discipline. When Titi was punished for disobeying orders one day, she cried all the way home and told her parents that she was not going back to school. End of school, end of punishment and end of trouble. Nothing her parents said about school made any sense to her. Anybody who liked the treatments in the school could go through the pain to become a doctor, lawyer or whatever her parents meant. As for her, it was a "don't-go area!" In fact, it was danger zone to her. It was about eleven years later that Titi began to appreciate what her parents were trying to tell her about schools. She became deficient in so many areas. She was almost persecuted for not having the basic education even among her peer groups. Her friends would exchange story books and gathered to retell and analysis them. Whenever she requested them to tell her the story in the book they have read, they would simply give her the book and said, 'you can read it yourself. Nobody has got the time to tell you any story.' It was as if they always deliberately subjected her to ridicule since they all knew she could not read and write.

    She was frustrated enough to tell her parents that she would like to go back to school. Her parents who were still conscious of what the witch doctor told them consented to her decision. So Titi began her elementary education at the time many of her friends were already graduating from high schools. The insults she had to endure as the oldest student in the school were more than enough to discourage her. The students nicknamed her as "Grandma in the school" or "old Rabbit in the small hole." Her determination to get education was strong enough to make her tolerated the names she was called in the school. She would rather endure the names than the persecution among her age group or the pains of being labeled as illiterate.

Things turned out well when she got to the high school where she met Bamidele Moore, her English teacher who later became her husband.

Bamidele was a gentleman to the core. Because of his Christian background, he was very reluctant to go into a relationship with one of his students even though he was in love with her the first few days he was her teacher. He could not help paying close attention of Titi who did not look like a student to him but a very beautiful young lady who was denied the opportunity to go to school early. To at least satisfy his love for her, he did all he could do to help her make up for the years she had lost before starting her formal education. Titi was so eager to learn that before anyone knew it, she was far ahead her classmates, making it possible for her skip two classes before she completed the high school education. If she was in love with Bamidele who contributed tirelessly and tremendously to her education, she did not know nor showed it except that she made it obvious to him that he was sent to her by God. This might be due to her inferiority complex. She considered him an icon of knowledge that could never go wrong, no matter what other people said or thought of him. So showing it to him in any way that she was in love with him was absurd, if not total madness. He, on the hand, sought for the opportunity to express his love that was growing by the day but it appeared there was none.

One day, shortly before she graduated from the school, he sought for her audience which she eagerly gave to him. They met alone in his quarters in the school compound. That was a risk as the school authority did not permit a female student to meet a male teacher alone in his quarters. It was a risk he was willing to take anyway. For one, he could not afford to let the lady he loved to slip away without telling her how much he felt about her. Secondly, in a few days from the day they met, she would cease to be as a student in the school and that, to a large extent, gave her the freedom to meet with anyone she pleased. If the school has problem with the relationship with a lady of marriageable age, the management could as well go to the State Ministry of Education to complain. He was going to make a marriage proposal to Titi and that was it. They were never involved in any relationship let alone getting involved in sex. He could readily prove it if there was need.

As soon as Titi stepped into his living room, she could almost perceive what was coming though she was not so sure. The food and

6

the soft drinks he had specially prepared for just two of them sent a signal of his intention.

He ushered her to the dinning table with a smile.

Pretending not to be suspicious, she followed him to the table. He offered a prayer which she could not really recall but she remembered he said something like, 'Lord, be our guide in everything we are going to do or say today.'

She said her amen but she was eager to hear it. He did not say much as they took the meal. Her mind raced, thinking ahead what he intended to say or do.

At last, after what appeared like eternity, after they silently took the meal, he cautiously led her to a couch and gestured her to sit down. He sat opposite her.

She did not directly look at him except to occasionally steal a glace at him so as to read his thoughts. At that time, she still considered him to be almost an angel and not a potential lover.

'Well,' he said, smiling at her for a thousand and one times, 'you do observe that I'm not treating you as my student any more, don't you?'

She simply nodded silently, looking at her hand bag - the old fashioned type she snatched from her mother when she was going out on a special occasion.

'Do you know the reason?'

She shook her head without saying a word.

'You want me to tell you the reason?'

She nodded silently. Actually she did not plan to make it hard for him to woo her if that was what he wanted from her but he did not make things easier for her either by keeping her waiting endlessly. So she felt the need to play the game of hard-to-catch. It would not only make the moment pleasant and memorable but also make her see how much he valued her.

'Well, you're a lady - a beautiful one, not a girl,' he said, looking at her face.

'Really, sir?' She looked back at him and looked away almost immediately. She was obviously happy that he pointed that out.

He nodded, still smiling. In fact he was smiling through out the conversation except the time he discovered that she was about to play prank.

'Yes,' he said. 'You're a lady. By the way, how old are you?'

She forced herself to look at him. Of course, by then she was getting surer of what he was up to.' You mean you don't know?'

7

He shook his head. 'I don't really know. If there's anything you think I know, it's mere guess.'

'What's your guess?' she asked, not feeling the need to be courteous now. Actually she was giving him signal that she was about to play the game of hard-to-catch.

'I guess you're twenty-three.'

'Well, I'm twenty- two,' she told him. 'How about you, sir?'

'This discussion is about you, not me - isn't it?' He said softly.

'I think discussion is a two-way street except if you want to tell me I'm in the classroom where only the teacher asks questions and the students give answers like zombies.'

Now he realized from the tone of her voice that she was about to play the tough lady. He knew, of course, that she was a bluff. He knew she would not refuse him if he offered to marry her. What made him so sure was not really clear.

'I maintain it, honey,' he said calmly, thinking that, at least, the pet name would make it obvious that he was about to woo her. 'This discussion is about you, not me. But we can make it a two-way discussion only if you first give me all the facts I need about you.'

There was a brief thoughtful silence between them.

'Mr...' She attempted to be formal.

'Call me Bamidele if you don't mind,' he interrupted.

'I do mind, sir,' she said with a snort. 'You know students are not taught in the school to address their teachers that way.'

'This discussion is between two of us. Leave the school out of it.' His smiles were fading now. It was necessary to make them fade just to pretend as if he was getting impatient with her.

'All right,' she conceded reluctantly. He was to prove it to her later that his intelligence was by far superior to hers, making her to realize that her game was like a childish play of a house cards. 'You have access to my file in school, don't you?'

'Yes... So?'

'You don't need to ask me anything about myself, including my date of birth, my parents and even where live if that's all you want to know.'

'Don't you think that would be intruding if I get all these facts about you through your file? Besides that, I don't think I have to go that far before I get what I need from you, knowing fully well what I mean to you and what you mean to me.' The game was about to come to an end even before she had the time to prepare for it.

There was a long silence that made him confident but it made her

8

uncomfortable. She decided to lay down the card she considered a joker. She said, 'I don't know I mean anything to you and I'm not sure you mean anything to me.' That was technically true but he did not believe it.

His smiles faded completely. He slowly stood up to pace round in front of her, pretending to be hurt though he was thinking of how to force her to admit that she loved him. 'How do you expect a man who cared for you for at least three years to be informed that he means nothing to you?'

'I don't mean that…'

He waved her to silence and went to sit again. This time she was bordered about the expressions on his face though as she later realized, they were all coercions and means to get on her kneels. 'Don't make me feel that the three years I invested in your life are all wastes.'

'Remember, sir, you did it for others too,' she said. 'Don't make me feel that you did all these for something.'

He shot a glance at her. She mistook the looks for something else. She thought she had said something wrong again but he actually viewed it as a sense of courage and knowledge. To test her intelligence further, he asked, 'what do you mean by that?'

'I … I mean no harm…'

'I don't mean what you don't mean,' he said firmly.

'You're getting me confused,' she confessed. 'You brought me here to fight me, sir?'

'Oh, no…'

She could see signs of regret on his face which she considered as scores of points. She wanted more points. So she said, 'if that's not the case, then you probably want me to pay for what you sowed into my life for three years.'

'On, no Titi….'

In a sober reflection, she asked, 'then what do you want from me, sir?'

He looked away. He had seriously underestimated her reasoning power. He had to throw in the towel now if he did not want her to get a wrong impression about him. 'I would have told you this long before now, Titi, but I can't. It's not because I think you're too young then but because I want you to complete your studies.' He looked at her. 'You're very special to me. For those years, I hide it and I never treat you specially or differently.'

'What makes me special or different from the rest?' she asked softly.

'I... love you.'

She smiled. 'We all know you love everybody. We always admire you for that. Through out the period we were in schools, you're regarded as the best teacher. We love you too. I remember when one of the naughty boys said one nasty thing about you, the rest of the class ganged up against him.'

'What is it he said?'

'We promised him we'll never tell you when he apologized.'

'But one of you told me,' he said. The smiles were coming back now and that was making her feel comfortable again. 'He said I used to take the girls to bed, especially you, being the most matured among all the students.'

She looked puzzled. 'You mean you know this all the while?'

He nodded. 'I don't blame him actually. He must have noticed you're much more attracted to me than the rest of the students though I tried hiding it from everyone. When he made that statement, I was not angry or surprised at all. The boy only sees what you or others didn't see. He probably foresees the time I'll take you to the Church for marriage and then take you to bed where we'll form all the babies in the world.'

For a long time, she gaped at him, wondering if he was joking or not. The expression on his face which did not change told her he was not joking at all. She suddenly burst out into hysterical laughter. 'Who is going to have all the babies in the world for you?'

He replied quickly, 'you!'

'Can you afford to take care of all the babies in the world with your poor pay packet?'

He could see that was a way of saying, "yes" to his proposal. 'We'll start with one, then two, three and four. If they are eating out our lives we'll stop there.'

Titi was never the same since Bamidele proposed to marry her. Their families readily supported their marriage which yielded two males and one female. Richard who was the first child was about twenty years old, Tope who was a girl of sixteen was the second and Femi who was fourteen years was the last of the children.

The family was blissfully set up in Ibadan, one of the largest cities in Nigeria. Titi through her small scale business venture always brought in some money that was used to cater for a few things in the home while Bamidele who was a vice principal in a public school till the day he died in a car accident bore the major responsibility in the

10

family. When he died, things fell apart in the family but Titi was able to meet up with the responsibilities in the family through the full payment of his gratuity by the government and the payment made by a life insurance company. A large part of the money went into completion of the family house where they resided while the rest went into her business, schooling and feeding the remaining members of the family.

Now that Richard was going into the university - a world that was different from what he was brought up with, she feared he might be influenced to join the bad wagons that were rampant in nearly all Nigerian campuses. She, therefore, felt the need to see him in his room that midnight and remind him of whom he was. He must be reminded that he needed to focus on his career he was about to build as a civil engineer which his father always dreamt for him. Since he was so promising and the only hope the family has to be relieved of her financial burden, she must tell him again and again that he must not let her down. He must abide by the Christian moral principles and family values which she and his father have built in him and other children.

She stood up clumsily from the bed to go and see him in his room.

CHAPTER TWO

Richard slept soundlessly on his bed in his room. The room was a little dark though one could see through the moonlight that reflected through the window. It was tidy and clean. As there was always power failure in the area, he always kept the window opened for fresh air anytime he was in the room. All the four bedrooms and the sitting room were well ventilated. The windows were all made up of glass louvers and secured from the outside with burglar proofs and mosquito nets. So he could afford to open the window all day long.

Titi opened the door silently and switched on the light. Richard did not move. He was sound asleep. She went to sit on the edge of his bed and tapped him gently.

Richard woke up with a start and asked sleepily, 'Mum, what do you want at this hour?'

She hesitated for a while before she said in a quiet voice, 'I want to talk to you and I don't want to do that when everybody is awake. So I decided to wait till now.'

Richard yawned and sits up, leaning against the wall and using the pillow to cushion his back. 'I'm sure it's very important.'

'It is,' she replied. 'It has to do with your admission into the University.'

'What about it?'

'The stories I heard about campuses frighten me. I was told there are different kinds of groups in most of our universities and they include secret cults and other bandwagons,' she said in whispers and almost in a state of panic. 'With your temper, I fear you're vulnerable to... to... I don't want you to mix up with any gang. That's the bottom line.'

He took a deep breath before he let it out and the said, 'I wish I know what you are worried about. I've told you that you don't have to worry about anything. I'm capable of making the right decisions.'

'You think you have what it takes to control your mood and be a man but you're not,' she said. 'You could still be influenced. I wish you run your program on part-time but you said your uncle wants you to do it on full time.'

He looked bored. 'Mum, do we have to go through all these again? I mean I can't recall how many times we've talked about this.'

'You don't understand, my dear...'

'Perhaps if you explain, I'll understand what exactly is bordering you.'

'I'm afraid…' She said reluctantly, 'I have a premonition that you will be influenced by some gangs. So I feel I should not only tell you but also emphasize the fact that you're our only hope of getting out of the unpleasant financial condition in this family… You know what I've gone through since your father died? I did all I could to get you and other children the best I can afford. We… I mean your two brothers, your sister and I are counting on you to relieve us of poverty....' Suddenly, the thought of his father invaded her mind and before she knew it she had burst into sobs.

Of course, Richard who knew her mother to be very sensitive guessed at once that the memory of his father must have flashed in her mind. She always saw him as a carbon of his father. Hence she counted so much on him to be the father of his younger ones.

Richard cuddled his mother and said, 'it's okay, mum, you don't need to worry about me … I'll not let you down.'

She looked at him with hope. 'Is that a promise?'

'Yes.'

*   *   *   *   *

The Black skull members were holding a meeting in the dark night at one of the remote areas around the campus of the university. The cult was made up of many young men though most of them do were not allowed to attend certain meetings like the one they were holding that night.

The members of the Black skull who usually dressed in black when they were operating were categorized into three major groups during her inception as a secret cult on campus. A group which was the one holding meeting now was the executive class. It was made up top members, ranging from the Capo, the over all leader to the executive spies who gathered information about the activities of the school and the students, including executive members of other cults.

13

This group also has as her members, the commandoes who made offensive or defensive move against the enemies of the cult. The enemies were usually those that refused to join the group after becoming their victims or after they were discovered to be working against the interest of the cult. Examples of those working against The Black Skulls were the spies working for The Red Eyes, an equally giant and vigilante cult.

There were other top members in the executive class like the herald guys who normally got items like money, weapons and drugs for the cult through a secret network with fellow cult members in other institutions, dirty police officers, unscrupulous government officials and politicians that often times engaged the illicit services of campus cults to achieve their political ambitions.

The second group within the cult was the secret members. These members occupied sensitive positions in the school which were very vital in the operations of the cult. Such membership cut across students and even lecturers. The cult communicated and gave assignments to them through the spies who knew most, if not all of them. The third group which was also made up of secret members was usually ex-members who graduated from the University or those who were highly placed in the society like the business tycoons, so-called philanthropies and so many others who were in the corridors of powers like in State Government Houses and the Presidential Villa in Abuja known as Aso Rock.

The Black skull was one of the oldest and the most well organized secret cults in Nigerian tertiary institutions. The cult was so powerful and dreadful that the name often sent most students on campus into hiding. The members could cause bloodbaths in any place, at any time and go away with it. If any of them was caught, he was always declared innocent or a victim once the Capo made one or two phone calls. What actually gave the Block Skull so much power was their connections with the political power houses and access to money and weapons through their godfathers.

It was hard to trace the origin of the Black Skull but going by the operations and the objectives of the cult, it was assumed that it originated from the secret cult from outside the campus among highly placed and wealthy people who used the youths to carry out certain dirty works, which they could not afford to be associated with. Such dirty works included assassinations of political rivals, rigging of elections, kidnaping, supplies of human beings for ritual killings or sacrifices and other forms of atrocities.

The Black Skull has become monstrous since the time it was introduced somewhere around 1990s - about the time the military government was in power. It was at this time that cultism was becoming very rampart in tertiary institutions even though it has been in existence as early 1960s if not earlier. The issue of cultism on campus has grown out of the control of the so-called founding fathers. It has now become more or less like network of deadly syndicates that was much more organized than the old mafia in Italy and other countries. Because it has become diabolical with some of them going into sorceries, it has become much more powerful and dreadful than what the founding fathers conceived it.

The Black Skull was almost like an evil agent that has powerful people as their clients. In fact, many of those in the third group within the cult were their clients. Just like in the normal business transactions, the cult often entered into unholy agreements before any contract was informally entered into. Such contract may involve a politician who wanted his rival to be assassinated with the promise to fund the cult for a certain period. It may also involve a businessman who wanted his business partner to be eliminated, often because he wanted to take the whole profit in a business deal.

The Black Skulls never felt the need to be loyal to anyone or other cults, going by their slang which indicated that the blood and flesh of people outside the cult meant nothing to them. The cult had been involved in so many atrocities that resulted in bloodshed and brutalities. With the growth of all secret cults in Nigerian campuses at large, their activities had become so complex that nobody can claim to be an authority in the ways each operated. They have grown into cancerous monsters that threatened the entire system of the whole nation. They turned into battlefields the institutions that were established with the objectives to empower youths with skills, grooming them into responsible citizens and future leaders. Many parents were now scared to let their children go through the institutions. As if that was not enough to threaten the peace of the country, the activities of the cults were spreading to people of other walks of life, including skilled, unskilled labourers, professionals and religious fanatics like the Boko Haram that were bombing the nation down with high explosives. With the efforts of the government which seemed quite inadequate, the cults were at first forced to go into hiding for a while as many people clamoured for the total eradication of these vice rings. What looked like a healed breast cancer in the motherland was actually spreading silently and secretly to other parts of her body. Before anyone knew it, the monsters were already in secondary and even primary schools all over the country, especially government owned schools. The cults not only operated on campus but also made initiations of new members their priorities over every other things. They often send agents to secondary schools to influence the students either with money or diabolical powers to become members of secret cults. All they needed to do to spread their tentacles was to get a hooligan who has the potential to lead the cult in the school, initiate him, train him on what to do and then empower him with money and sometimes with weapons or charms. The hooligan would mobilize others to form a cult in the school. The formation could be immediate or gradual, radical or subtle, depending on the tolerance of the authority or ways of enforcing discipline in the school. With the cult frame work in secondary schools, it was always easy for the secret cults on campuses to enlist their members when the secondary school students gained admissions into tertiary institutions. All they needed to do to get their members was to look for any sigh of hooliganism in the students.

The costs of operations and functions of most of the cults on campus were always quite enormous. So they needed a lot of funds. Because most, if not all the cults were funded by powerful people that awarded them unscrupulous and atrocious contacts like supplies of ladies for prostitution or ritual killings, members were always encouraged to be involved in the nefarious activities. In fact most of the cults were always trying to prove more ferocious and powerful than the others through the deeds that often shocked the entire world. While trying to prove superiority to one another, they got involved in series of conflicts that often resulted into bloodshed of both members and innocent students. No matter how much the society tried to fight it, it was like fighting a large army of invisible soldiers. A cult member could be so gentle and even dedicated in the Church that whenever investigation revealed that he or she was the faceless enemy, arguments and even quarrel became the order of the day. Many students often slept and woke up the following day only to find out that one of their friendly neighbours was dead in his room. Investigations by the police would reveal that he was a warrior in a cult.

The Black Skulls, as the members of the ruthless and deadly cult on campus were called, were having their first meeting while the University was just resuming for the new academic year.

The Capo, as the leader was called, was a twenty- eight year old man called Banjo. He presided over the meeting that night.

Banjo was regarded by people that knew him as a devil incarnate though no one needed to be told that he must be really ferocious. His election as the leader of such deadly cults was enough to tell everyone on campus that he was really a cruel guy. He was studying Biochemistry and currently a three hundred level student even though he ought to have graduated two years ago. He deliberately carried over six courses just to retain his post as the Capo of the dreadful Black skulls, enjoying the power and the respect accorded to him.

He climbed into the elevated position of the cult leader after he committed chain of atrocities that terrified the students in the entire campus. When he was first admitted into the University, nobody ever suspected that he would pose a serious threat to many lives. Actually, he was bred by his father who was a member of an appealing but deadly cult called Brotherhood Fraternity. Although his father who was called Sanmilesan did not know or intend to encourage any of his nine children to be involved in occult practices. From his experiences so far, all secret cults were nothing but insanity which, once anyone was involved would prove nearly impossible to opt out. He was actually lured into it through a close friend when he was looking for a diabolical means to create wealth for himself. Before he knew cultism was not for any sane person like him, he was already neck deep in it. Although he benefitted tremendously from his involvement in Brotherhood Fraternity, he also paid dearly for it later. When he turned seventy, he considered what he went through in life as nightmares and his wealth as vanities which amounted to nothing if he compared them with what he had lost.

Sanmilesan was a very promising and hardworking middle age man before he joined the cult. He had a tailoring business which the cult helped him to transform into a fashion and textile company shortly after he was initiated. At first, he enjoyed the money he was making through efforts of the cult, attracting a lot of women, including three of his wives who married him when he became wealthy. When he was later mandated to attend certain meetings at the cult main shrine where ritual killings normally took place, he knew he had made a mistake to have become a member. He began to witness first hand horror of secret cults in the country. It was then he realized that not every mad people in the society were actually mad and not every transporter or trader was real. There some people who were always placed at some areas in some towns with the intention to kidnap humans. They often times pretended to be mad people or transporters and petty traders. If any of them had contacts with their

17

victims through charms or other magic powers, it would take a miracle for any of them to escape. There were also executioners among the cult members who killed the victims after accessing their spiritual worth through demonic means. Of course, there were some victims that were considered untouchables. They normally returned the untouchables while the touchable ones were always butchered and dismantled like chicken. There were always buyers among cult members who were waiting to buy the human parts. They bought the heads, the hearths, the sex organs and sometimes the breasts of women.

Sanmilesan found it hard to leave the cult despite the horror which he later experienced. Since he knew the implications of frowning at the cult atrocities, he tried to get used to them, doing all he could to hide the atrocities he was involved in from his considerably large family. It soon dawned on him that it was almost impossible for vicious cult members to hide their true identities from those who lived with them. Through one item or activity or the other, his identity was revealed to some members of his family.

Banjo got to know that his father was a cult man when he was in Junior Secondary School. Being an inquisitive boy, he always found some strange items in his father's room. This led him to enter his strong room where he was holding a meeting with some of the cult members one day. The intrusion into the meeting made the cult leader to instruct Sanmilesan to present Banjo as member of the cult at the junior cadre. As if he was waiting for the opportunity, Banjo learnt all he could from the cult and proved it to the members that he would one day lead the cult. He knew the items the cult always needed and he always voluntarily contributed his part. Sanmilesan was shocked to discover that his boy could grow so ferocious within a short time to the extent that human lives meant nothing to him. In order to reduce his vicious activities, he tried to divert his attention to the school where he did not know hosted a lot of secret cults.

It was easy for Banjo to find all the existing secret cults on campus being a cult guy himself. He sought out the most ruthless ones among them. He found The Black Skulls to be the most vicious. He joined the cult and aimed to be the leader.

Becoming the Capo of The Black Skulls was a lot easy for him. All he had to do to prove to his worth was to eliminate most of the leaders of revival cults and presented their heads to the Capo of the Black skulls at that time. He stated it point blank at the meeting that if he has no strong leader to lead him, he would have to come for the head of the Capo as he could not afford to let weak leader lead him in the cult. Instead of stepping down for Banjo, the Capo expelled himself from the school that year, using the expulsion to save his face. Banjo was unanimously elected the Capo of the Black skulls.

Banjo sat on his chair at the meeting that was taking place at one of the hideouts of the cult. He looked thoughtful as he stood up. The rest of the members stooped on the ground. It was obvious how much they feared and respected him.

'The Black Skulls!' Banjo said suddenly.

The rest chorused, 'brotherhood is life but the flesh, the blood and the bones of others are nothing!'

'We've had a lot of our members graduating from this institution,' the Capo said. 'Many of them are already in business, in politics, in government or in the corridor of powers. All of them have at one time or the other pledged their loyalties to The Black Skulls. Hence we can count on them for their supports and they can count on us to help them achieve their aims either through threat and intimidation or other forms of violence.

'As you know that the strength of a legion does not only depend on its tactics and weaponry but on its number… If we must not fail in all our missions, there is need for fresh hands in our team, we need more strength and….'

'Strengths come in numbers!' The cult members responded.

'Since you are all conscious of this,' he continued, 'you will agree with me that with the graduation of six of our fine members from this school, the strength of The Black Skulls is reduced. We need to recover our strength soonest if we want to remain relevant on campus and the outside world. How do we go about this?' He paused for a while, walking round the men who were mostly in their early twenties. 'The institution has just resumed for the new session and many new students are expected to be on the campus soon. So every member is mandated to recruit at least three students into the great cult....'

'The Black Skulls!' The rest chorused again.

'We need as many as are courageous or masculine or intelligent. This must be done with enough passion that guarantees success. Use whatever it takes to bring them in. Provoke if you have to, brutalize if you have to but don't kill. We are not at war yet. We are simply recruiting....'

CHAPTER THREE

Richard Moore came out of the administrative blocks, looking uncertain. He had gone to the office with the hope that he would be able to complete the first registration process into the State Government University that offered him an admission to study civil engineering. He was referred to the engineering department that needed to complete a section in the registration form before it could be received from him.

He looked round the unfamiliar place, seeking for any friendly looking student that might be kind enough to direct him since he was not sure how to find his way to the place. This was the hundred and one times he was going to miss his way. The locations of all the departments were so identical and confusing that he felt stupid. If not for the help of his cousin who was a two-hundred level student in the science department, he would have found it very hard to find his bearing. He had assured him, however, that he only needed to spend few days on campus before he got used to where all the blocks, including the classrooms were located.

Unlike his late father who has gentle personality, Richard Moore was a strong willed young man in his early twenties. He has a well built statue with the looks of a determined athlete. He was actually an athletic because of his interest in boxing. He was always fascinated by the sport, making him to associate with some boxers that lived in the neighbourhood. He often times trained with them though his mother clamoured against it. 'Do you want to be a street fighter and bring problems into the family?' His mother would often times ask him whenever she saw him returning from training.

'I'm not planning to be a street fighter,' he would reply her at times. 'It's a sport I enjoy.'

'You enjoy fighting?' she asked one day, expecting a serious debate on the matter. 'What's your interest in fighting? What do you enjoy in that? I know of only one set of people that enjoys fighting.

They are called thugs!'

He dared not argue with her if he did not want to see her tears. She had always used the untimely death of his father as a tool to enforce order in the house. So he sometimes sneaked out to train with the boxers only when he knew he would not be caught.

Studying Civil Engineering had always been the dream of his father though he did not know why he wanted him to be an engineer. When he was in secondary school, his father would tell him about his friend who was a building contractor and how much he made success in the job. He did not have to tell him that he wished that Richard, being his first child, took it as a profession. Before he expressed the dream, he had decided that he would be a Civil Engineer.

No doubt, he respected and loved his father. He was a real gentle and intelligent man. His philosophies which he must have read in books or developed by himself have tremendous impact in all the children's ways of thinking. Through him, he was able to understand so many things about life. With the influence he had on all the children, he was able to enforce discipline and at the same time proved to them that he was ready to sacrifice anything to ensure that their future was well secured. The impact he made in the lives of his children was so much that even after his death, his mother used his life to get a firm grip over them. She was always saying, 'your father would have said....' Then she would say her mind, which might not necessarily conform to their father's opinion. At times, she would say, 'I know your father would have told you to do "this or that".' All these were just ways of using his influence in them to get things done the way she wanted.

Though when he died, things were not so bad financially for the family. The money he left behind was enough to carry on with life for years without him but the psychological effect in every member of the family was enormous. Richard knew how much his mother loved and relied on his father. So he played a great role in bringing out the family out of the gloom and promised to take the challenge of life where his father stopped. He even quoted his father who said, "Problem is not a problem until you see it as a problem. Likewise, solution as unrealistic as it may seem can be solution to your mental state if you see it." He would never forget the smiles on his mother's face, making all the children that were with them to smile as well. His mother looked relieved. She even said, 'your father is not really dead. He's still inside you. That's very comforting.' Through out the gloomy period, the philosophies of his father kept coming to his mind, which he always repeated to the family. That served them as consolations. Before anyone realized it, the family was back on her feet within a short time.

Another problem emerged again, however, which reminded them of the responsibilities of his father. It has to do with Richard university education. He wanted to study civil engineering as his father desired but the family was short of fund now. A lion share of the money they got from the government as his father's gratuity has gone into building the family house. Again, he remembered the wise words, as quoted many times by his father, "once there is will, there is a way." He told himself, 'it is the strength of my will that will make way for me." So he went straight to one of his uncles whom he knew could afford to sponsor him in the university. He had logics and weapon of persuasions handy before he went to his uncle for the discussion about his education. When he got to his house, he was not around. He had gone to hold a meeting with his business colleagues. He was into the business of agricultural products and services. He has twelve fish ponds and about thirty acres of palm tree farm at Egbe, their home town. The uncle was popularly known as Chief T. J Moore. He was considerably rich, going by the way poor people defined the word "rich". To most people around then, anyone who has a business that was big enough to cater for so many things was considered rich. In the real sense of it, however, Chief T. J Moore was not so rich. At least, the real rich people never considered him so. What actually made him won the respect of both rich and poor people was his large heart. He was always willing to help those who were really desperately in need of his help. People in Chief T. J Moore's class were always considered poor, no matter their income, going by the adage in the society that implies, "a rich person with a large heart in the midst of multiple of needy people is in fact the poorest among them all."

When Richard met him hours later, after his cousins and mother had made him felt at home, Chief T.J asked him straightaway if there was problem. 'I know you must have a good reason for waiting for so long to see me,' he said, sitting together with him in a reasonably well furnished sitting room.

'You're... em... right, sir,' Richard answered reluctantly. 'I'm having s a little problem, sir.'

'Aaha! Problem? Let's hear the problem you call little, my dear,' he said, taking some juice drinks which he normally drank before he had his meal.

'It has to do with my education, daddy,' Richard said courteously. It was customary in the ethnic group of Yoruba to address uncles who are old enough to be one's father as father. Besides that, the brother of a deceased man often stood as a father of the children of the deceased. In fact, in some spectacular cases, the brother may be mandated to marry the wife of the deceased.

'Why coming to border me about your education,' he said. 'I thought my brother left you some money to take care of yourself. He used to tell me that the government would pay him a lot of money when he retired. What happens to all the money?'

'We … em spend it, sir.'

'Oh, my God!' He pretended to be shocked. 'What did you do with that kind of money?' he asked as if he didn't know.

'We built a house, sir,' Richard said.

'Oh....'

'I thought my mother told you, sir.'

'She didn't, my dear.'

'She told me she sent someone to you to tell you after trying to see you ….'

'See, see,' Chief T. J said, waving at him indifferently. 'Actually, I heard this at the family meeting which you are supposed to attend but choose not to. I don't know why.'

'I didn't know the time. I'm sorry, sir.'

'Let's not talk about that,' he interrupted. 'Since she is my brother's wife, she's also my wife. If she single-handedly takes decisions since the death of my brother without consulting the family, she is telling me that I'm not relevant in her life and yours too.'

'That's not true, sir!'

'Let me tell you what the truth is, young man,' he told him, looking stern. 'Your mother was brought into the family of Moore but you and the rest of the children were born inside. Her attitude is nothing short of sign of autonomy.'

'I should be blamed for that attitude, sir,' Richard said gently, feeling the need to defend his mother, 'if that is the impression about her.'

'Why?' he shot at him.

'I can say I influence her decisions,' he replied softly. 'I didn't know that's not the way we should go about things. I'm sorry, sir.'

'She ought to know better than making decisions with you. Tell me, what do you know?'

'Nothing, sir,' he whispered.

'Well,' Chief T J continued, 'the family would have come to interfere with the business of my brother which you take so personally but I stopped them. I knew sooner or later, you're going to call for our help. We didn't wait for so long before you come. See?'

'I'm sorry, sir. We didn't know you're offended by the things we do on our own. But you never show it to us in anyway. You played the role of a father and… em….'

'That is my customary duty,' he said. 'I didn't allow anyone to show his grievances either because somehow we have no reason to question the way you spend your father's money. If it's not sound, we'll have come in. Of course, I just want you to realize that the attitude is wrong and no family member is interested in taking what is rightfully yours.'

Richard prostrated. 'Thank you for forgiving us, sir.'

'You're forgiven even before you ask for it.'

Richard sat down again. 'Thank you, sir.'

'I don't want you to tell your mother a thing. After all, she's just a woman. Though she's a member of our family, she can't represent your father. Only you can.'

Richard bowed and repeated. 'Thank you, sir.'

'About your school,' Chief T. J said. 'I don't want to pretend as if I don't know about it. Wole told me about it.'

Richard hid his surprise. Wole was his cousin, Chief's second son who was giving him information about the admission into the University. He didn't really expect him to tell his father about it because he told him it was a secret which no one, not even his mother knew about.

'He told me because he wants you to be in his school,' Chief T. J explained as if he could read his thoughts. 'He wants me to talk to a professor friend of mine about your admission.'

Richard was glad to note that his cousin meant well after all.

'The problem, as you know, is not getting you admitted into the University. The problem is: it's expensive. You know that State owned Universities are getting too expensive for an average Nigerian parent to afford these days. So let me ask you: who is going to foot the bill?'

Richard was silent.

'I see,' Chief T. J said, smiling. 'You're hoping I would, aren't you?'

Richard stole a glace at him. He caught his smiles. He was encouraged. Returning the smiles, he said, 'I know I still have a father that is capable.'

Chief T. J laughed. 'You're as smart as your dad. You think you can shave my head behind me? Boy, I'll tell you the truth, I can't guarantee you I can afford to give you a full sponsorship, considering what's on my neck already. Besides, if I do that, your brothers and sister will expect me to do the same for them.'

'You have to give me the full scholarship, daddy,' Richard said firmly. 'I have no one else to turn to.'

'Can't you understand the point, son?'

'No, sir. I don't.'

'I'm full to the neck with responsibilities. My children need investments so do my business. There are lots of projects in my hands which I cannot execute for lack of fund. That's not to talk of other members of the family I have to help.' He paused for a while, expecting him to respond. When he didn't, he said, 'I'll give you half of everything you'll need in the school every session while your mother takes care of the rest. Is that okay, son?'

'No, sir. What's left with us is reserved for our welfare and the secondary school education of the rest of the children.'

'Your mother had trading business she's doing, isn't it?'

'It's the income in business she uses to take care of what we need in the house, including the school fees of the rest. Taking the things I need in the school out of the business will kill the business.'

Chief T. J looked thoughtful for a while. 'So what are we going to do now?'

'I don't know, sir,' Richard answered quietly, 'except that I know I must go to the University to study civil engineering as my father desired.'

'I will think of another way. Give me time, okay?'

'Can I ask you a question, sir?' Richard said, ready to touch the large heart which everybody knew he has.

'Go ahead.'

'Would your decision be different if I'm Wole?'

He stared at him for a long time.

Richard felt so uncomfortable that he looked down on the floor, uncertain if he had asked the right question.

After a while, he said, 'it's a big question, son. I honestly can't answer that.'

He could see that he had scored a point. He wanted to score another one. So he asked, 'can I ask another question, sir?'

'Why not if it's not like the one I can't answer?'

'I have to be candid, sir. You're a very transparent father. I think I would like to emulate the honesty in you.' He paused for a while and shrugged. Then he said, 'the reason I'm asking this question is to know what I and my younger ones really mean to you. Since you don't seem to know, I have to ask another question. If I have the information I need, I would know how to relate with you. Actually, I don't mean to be a burden to you...'

'Don't go into that now,' Chief T. J said. He was getting a little uncomfortable at the trend of the discussion. He was beginning to feel the need to erase the wrong impression which his nephew was having about him. 'Just ask the question. I'll see if I can answer it.'

'What would my late father have done if he were to be in your shoes and if Wole were to be in my shoes?'

There was another very uncomfortable silence between them before Chief T. J said, 'okay, son, you win.' He added almost immediately, 'Boy, you're really mean!'

Richard laughed, forcing him to smile at him.

'I'll give you the full scholarship if that's the basis for all these troubling questions,' he told him. 'But there is a "but". You have to let your mother and your brothers and sister know from onset that I can't afford to sponsor any other children. When you graduate by God's grace, I'll get you a job. Through that you can help the rest. Is that okay?'

Richard felt so happy that he prostrated, saying, 'thank you so much, daddy. You're really a father.'

With the help of Wole and his uncle's connection, Richard was able to secure the admission into the university to study civil engineering. After the admission, Wole helped him to secure an accommodation outside the campus. He also assisted him in starting the registration process in the school. Now he had to continue the process without him as he was not available.

Richard looked round at the students who were either walking briskly in and out of the building or talking in groups. He hoped he would not appear stupid if he asked where to find the engineering department. After hesitating for a while, he saw a gentle looking man around twenty-five, giving everybody a piece of paper each. He wondered what was in the paper. Curiously, he waited for the man to get close to him. He did not need to ask for a copy before he stretched out his hand to give him.

'Would you like to have this?' he asked with a smile.

Richard took it from him and glanced through it curiously. It was a Christian tract titled: "Behold Your Power Of Choice Can Destroy You." He looked at him and said, 'thanks.... em...'

The man stopped to look at him when he noticed the inquisitive expressions on his face.

'Can you tell me where the Engineering Department is?' Richard managed to ask.

The man who later introduced himself as Lekan Akinsola was quick to notice he was a fresh student. 'You're a new student?'

Richard nodded silently.

'Come with me. I'll take you to the place,' Lekan told him. 'I hope you don't mind if I give these tracts to people we meet on the way.'

'Oh, no, I don't,' he replied. 'I'll wait.'

'You don't have to wait. I'll be giving them on the way,' Lekan said.

They walked only a few minutes before Lekan was engaged by a lot of people on the way.

Richard took the opportunity to read the tract.

"A man managed to send his son to the University to be trained as an Accountant but, on getting to the campus, he decided to join the cult even though he had the privilege to join any of the Christian fellowships around. Not thinking of the sacrifices his parents were making so that he could become an Accountant, he got involved in series of atrocities that were enough to tarnish the name and the image of his entire family. A year before he graduated, his cult had conflict with revival cult. The conflict resulted into his death and the deaths of many other people. Instead of his struggling parents to have an Accountant that will elevate the poverty in the family, they were given the dead body of a cult member.

"The Bible says in 1 Corinthians 15:33, "be not deceived: evil company corrupts good habit." In other words, the group of people you have chosen as your friends can turn you into evil person even if you're from a good home. You may not have the privilege to pick your mother or father or family or country but you have the power to pick your friends among so many other things. Most importantly, you have the power to accept Christ into your life now or to reject him. The Bible makes us to understand in Romans 8:1 that there is no condemnation for you if you decide to have Christ in your life. If you reject him, however, you would walk according to the pattern of this world. Destruction is the end of it all.

"Jesus is waiting, knocking at the door of your heart. He is ready to deliver you from all your sins and the wrong choices you have made. He will deliver you also from evil company which you have kept for so long a time. I pray that you make the right decision now."

He was almost through reading everything in the tract when Lekan returned.

Lekan said, 'I'm sorry to keep you waiting.'

There's no need to feel sorry,' he replied quickly. 'In fact I'm engrossed in the story in the tract.'

'I see,' Lekan said. 'Let's go straight to the place now.'

'Is the story in this tract real?'

'Yes,' Lekan replied without hesitation. 'The incident took place in this school.'

'So it's true that secret cults are rampant on campuses.'

Lekan looked at him as if he was an alien. 'You think all the horrible news about campus cultism you hear on radio and television are cock and bull stories?'

'I really don't listen to bad news.'

'How would you appreciate good news if you don't hear bad news?'

'I'll rather take the good news and appreciate it.'

Lekan smiled at him. They met another set of people on the way as they walked. He went to distribute the tracts to them and went to join Richard again. He said, 'I didn't catch your name. I'm not sure I told you mine. I'm Lekan Akinsola.'

'I'm Richard Moore....'

He smiled at him and said, 'your other names sound like someone from the western part of the world.'

'I'm actually from Egbe in Kogi State. As I was told, giving foreign names to African children is a legacy of European colonization which is now tagged as modern civilization.'

'I see,' Lekan said, occasionally handing out tracts to the people who cared to take them from him. Of course, some of them snubbed him. He did not look offended or discouraged.

They were now getting close to the Department of Engineering. 'What are you studying now?'

Richard replied, 'Civil Engineering. What about you?'

'Sociology. I'm in 300 Level.'

'That's good. It means you would soon graduate.'

'Very soon someone would be telling you the same thing,' Lekan said. 'I remember my first day in the University. It was like few weeks ago even though it's now three years.' There was a brief silence. He was hoping to give another set of students the tracts but they took another direction. He looked at him after a while and asked, 'have you secured an accommodation in the school?'

'Yes. I have a cousin who is a student here. He helped me get a room in one place they called... em... Inner....'

He cut in, 'Inner Temple.'

'Yes. You know the place?'

'Sure. You get to know many places and many people if you're involved on campus evangelism like me.'

'Do you get paid for this job?' Richard asked suddenly, wondering what was motivating him to distribute the tracts with so much zeal and dedication.

Lekan laughed. 'Of course not!' He laughed the more when Richard looked puzzled. His question reminded him of what they were told at the campus fellowship meeting where the speaker, an anointed man of God spoke extensively about evangelism. He quoted Daniel Webster, a famous state man and prominent lawyer in the 18th century, saying, '… if the truth be not diffused, error will; if God and his word are not known and received, the devil and his works will gain the ascendancy; if the evangelical volume does not reach every hamlet, the pages of corrupt and licentious literature will." The teachings of the man of God were so powerful that most of those who attended the meeting did not feel the same. What actually moved him to be engaged so much in evangelism was the way he explain the passages in Mark chapter sixteen verses fifteen and sixteen. The passage was read like this: "and he said unto them, go ye into all the world, and preach the gospel to every creature. He that believeth and is baptized shall be saved; but he that believeth not shall be damned." According to the speaker, there were three crucial points in the passage which were: the need to go into the world, preaching the gospel to everybody and the two eternal destinations of individuals.

'A lot of things depend on our going,' the speaker told them. 'If we don't go into all the world which can be interpreted as wherever we find ourselves, many souls will damn the eternal consequence.

'There is a little story I can use to explain this. I'll tell you if you don't mind. An old man has a big house with plenty of rooms that accommodate billions of his people. One day, the enemy came to plant a time bomb in the house. Nobody knows when the bomb will explode and set the entire house ablaze. The old man who had gone on a journey to prepare another place for his people was informed of this time bomb. He sent messages to everybody in the house to get out of it to a place where he would come to take them to another place where there was bliss. Some people received this message but most of them did not. Instead of everybody who got the message to warn the rest of the impending explosion, most of them did not. Only few are busy passing the message around. Vast majority of the people live in comfort zone, enjoying all the things they could in the house. There were lust of the flesh, lust of the eyes and pride of life right in that house. All these things are what could easily trigger explosion. Soon there was massive explosion in the house which sent most of the people into fire. Those who received the message and followed the instructions of the old man were the only saved ones. They were taken to another place with many mansions. Rewards were given to those who were up and doing for the old man.

'No one really needs anyone to explain what the story means. I'm sure everybody understands it. I would explain it all the same for the sake of clarity of thoughts and to avoid misinterpretation. Of course, the big house is this world which the Bible talks about in first John chapter two verse fifteen to seventeen. The passage reads like this. "Love not the world, neither the things that are in the world. If any man loves the world, the love of the Father is not in him. All that is in the world, the lust of the flesh, and the lust of the eyes, and the pride of life is not of the father but is of the world. And the world passeth away, and lust thereof but he that doeth the will of God abideth for ever."

'The old man who went to prepared a place for his people is Jesus who said in the gospel according to Saint John chapter fourteen verses two and three, "In my father's house there are many mansions: if it were not so, I would have told you. I go to prepare a place for you. And if I go and prepare a place for you, I will come again, and receive you unto my self; that where I am, there ye may be also."

'Those who receive the message are the Christians. You would have expected all of them to share the message if they really know how crucial if is. It is very shocking to note that most of them don't share the gospel with the people. By not sharing the message of the Lord, Christians create hostile environment for themselves. When the environment becomes very hostile, they become vulnerable. Before they know it, those who are supposed to preach against sins begin to get involved in the very sinful acts. In another way round, those who are up and doing in sharing the message of the Lord insulated themselves against the things of this world. They are given special grace to function as servants of God. These are the ones who wait and trust in the Lord for all they need. The Bible says in the book of Isaiah chapter forty verse thirty-one, "But they that wait upon the Lord shall mount up with wings as eagles; they shall run, and not be weary; and they shall walk, and not faint." If you want the kind of strength God promises all His people, go about the Lord's business instead of getting entangled with the affairs of this world.

'I believe in my hearts that all of you in this school are not here for education alone but also to carry the message of the Lord to everybody in this campus....'

Lekan reflected all the man of God had said that motivated him to reach out to the people within the few minutes of silence between him and Richard.

Since Lekan had got a personal contact with Richard, he felt the need to further share the word of God with him. 'I wonder why you ask me the question,' he said after awhile.

'You do the work as if you're making something out of it,' Richard replied, still wondering at what motivate him to distribute the tracts.

'Jesus said we should be fishers of men.'

'I think it's about religion - isn't?'

'No, my brother,' Lekan said although he did not know how he could make him understand since he did not even sound like a devoted Christian. He, however, added, 'to influence people to come to Christ is my joy. God touches the hearts of people through the work. If we don't win people for Christ, the devil will convert them for himself. If we allow the devil to prevail in our midst, the environment would be hostile for us all. Therefore we must act.'

'That's true,' Richard said thoughtfully.

'Inner Temple area just like everywhere on campus is made up of different kinds of guys. It's up to you to pick the right guys as friends.'

'I don't intend to have any friends.'

'If you don't make friends, believe me, friends will make you. You can't avoid that. So it's better you make the right ones by yourself before bad ones make you their friend.' He pointed at a building. 'That's where you're going.' He stretched out his hand to shake his.

'Thanks, Lekan.'

'You're welcome.'

Richard began to walk towards the building.

'Don't forget, Richard, if you don't stand for something positive, you will fall for anything... And that may be negative...'

'I can see that you learn a lot of philosophies in your department!' Richard said aloud. 'Thanks anyway.'

'I hope to pay you a visit or someone will!'

But Richard was not listening. His mind was somewhere else.

CHAPTER FOUR

Sunday Junior Ayoola was sent by Capo of the Black skulls to meet with Mat, a representative of the same cult in another tertiary institution. They were to exchange information, drugs and money.

Sunday who shortened his full name into Sjay was member of the first group in the cult. He was more or less an errand and delivery guy of the Capo. He was not masculine like most of the members but he was smart and efficient in carrying out all his assignments.

When he came to the University to study Language Art, he was as simple if not naïve as many of the fresh students who were usually nicknamed: Johnny Just Come (JJC). His parents were poor but when he began to mix with guys from rich families, his lifestyle changed completely. He quickly learned how to take drugs though his friends who supplied him in abundance without having to pay for it. He soon learned how to trade in drugs withon campus and, in no time, he had become a drug addict. It was in the course of dealing with drugs that he came into contact with a member of the Black skulls. The Black Skull who has now left school made friends with him, telling him he wanted him to supply some drugs to his club in the school. Sjay would have stayed cleared of him if he knew the club in question was actually the secret cult called The Black Skulls. For one, everybody knew the Black Skulls as students' nightmares and broad daylight horror. Before he knew he was dealing with a member of the cult, he had been invited to the club meeting where for the first time he was faced with dreadful members of the Black Skulls. The man who brought him in had told other members so many things about him, including his connection with guys that dealt in drugs within and outside the campus. Since drugs served as part of the items the members needed to feel excited and stimulated, especially when going for a tough battle, Sjay was definitely a guy they needed in the cult. He dared not resisted them when he was told he would be initiated as a member of the cult.

The initiation was quite a horrible experience which he would never forget for the rest of his life. He was taken into the forest where there were different kinds of human skulls and other dreadful items of initiation, including a middle aged woman. The slim woman looked somewhat mentally deranged though she was made to look pretty and calm. Her hair was well plaited. She wore only pants which was a little transparent. Her breasts were little firm.

Sjay was ordered to make love to the woman in the presence of top members who have come to initiate him into the cult. That was not too difficult for him because he was a little high with dope. The woman was so docile and co-operative that he wondered if she was under spell. She removed her pants by herself, laid down as he bounced on her. When he finished making love to her, the Capo handed him a long danger and ordered him to stab her in the heart. That was when the horror began. Reluctantly, he stabbed the poor woman. As if that was not enough, some of her blood was taken in a calabash. One of the members that served as the priest pronounced curses inside the blood, saying that if he betrayed the cult in anyway, he would be haunted by the spirit of the dead woman until he killed himself. He was given the blood to drink. With trembling hands, he took the calabash and drank the blood. Since that day, he lives of human beings meant nothing to him.

Sjay took the white substance in a pack from Mat, examined it before he gave him the money.

Mat, a mean looking man around twenty-three counted the money. Satisfied that it was completed, he pocketed it.

Sjay weighed the pack of substance in his hand and asked, 'you're sure this stuff is up to two kilo?'

Mat glared at him before he bellowed in deep rough voice, 'don't give me that shit! I weighed the damn thing myself. So if your Capo finds it less, we'll conclude that you tamper with it. If you tamper with the stuff, you'll be sorry, man!'

Sjay grinned at him. 'Alright, my guy. What do you have for the messenger boy?'

'Man mi, tell your boss to give you part of the stuff!'

'He... em ... can't give me enough of that, you know. There are many guys vying for the same stuff.'

'You can buy extra for yourself then.'

'Money is not easy to come by, you know.'

'So is the stuff.'

Sjay looked disappointed, appealing to him with the expression on his face.

Mat dug his hand slowly into his pocket and brought out a small wrap and handed it to him.

Sjay looked happy. 'Thanks a lot.'

Mat looked irritated as Sjay grinned, moving backward towards the exit of the lonely lecture hall. 'Hey yo! Don't get used to the gift because I won't give you every time you ask for it, okay?'

Sjay relied, 'sure, my guy. Greetings to your Capo and the brotherhood!'

Mat waved indifferently without looking at him, walking out of the hall through another door. 'Get lost, man!'

* * * * *

Richard was in his room, reading when there was a knock on the door. He looked at the direction, wondering who was by the door. He really did not know who has come to look for him since he has no friend and was determined not to have any. He asked after a brief pause, 'who is it?'

'It's Jacob Otedolu. I'm a student in your department. Is that Richard?'

Richard curiously went to open the door when he heard the visitor mentioned his name. Of course, Jacob was a total stranger. Though he was well known in the entire faculty as strong member of the campus Christian fellowship, he was always on the quest to convert students into Christianity anytime he was free from lecture. He was so fervent and devoted to evangelism that other students wondered if he had time to read at all. His performance during examination, however, going by the result, was always outstanding. This convinced them that either his God must have helped him to write all the examinations for him or he must have been reading in the mid nights while others were sleeping. In any case, God must be serving him well as he claimed. If not, the results of all the examinations he has taken in the University so far could not have been so outstanding. Just as he used to tell the people, his examination results were proofs that the God he preached about was real. What really worked for him was not just spending time to read but his strong faith in Jesus. He believed in what the Bible says about the used of time as recorded in

Ecclesiastes chapter three verses one and two which says, "to every thing there is a season, and a time to every purpose under the heaven: A time to be born, and a time to die; a time to plant and a time to pluck up that which is planted." So he learnt how to plan and organize his life. He knew the time students normally lazed away their time and the time they read which often times varied from one student to another. He spent his free period to engage other students in discussion about Jesus. Having been doing that for well over a year, he seemed to know how to engage them in discussion about God and tactfully lead them to Christ. He had so much influence in many students that they nicknamed him as Pastor Friend.

Jacob Otedolu worked in conjunction with other students like Lekan Akinsola who informed him about Richard. How the evangelical Christian students operated was simple. They have people at various faculties and departments. If the Christian student in one department came across a student that needed to be followed up in another department, he or she would simply give necessary information about the convert to another Christian in that department. Though that the Christian could monitor or follow up the convert. The efforts of the evangelical students seemed to pay off as more and more students joined Students Christian fellowship on campus.

Jacob smiled at Richard and offered his hand in handshake. Richard took it silently, not sure whether to welcome him or not. Not that he was unfriendly but he had quite made up his mind not to mix up with any students in spite of what Lekan told him. He was really determined not to have any friends until he graduated from school, relating with only his cousin, the only person he could trust.

'Hi, Brother Richard Moore,' Jacob greeted him cheerfully.

Richard looked puzzled, wondering where and how he got his full names. He said slowly, 'do I know you?'

'No, actually,' Jacob replied, 'but I'm a 200 Level student in your Department.'

'I see….' Richard said, waiting for him to tell him how he got the information about him.

'You met a member of Campus Evangelical Team last week,' Jacob explained in a friendly tone.

'What about it?'

'Actually he told me about you.'

'What is the name of this person?'

Jacob replied, 'he's brother Lekan Akinsola. You remember him?'

35

Richard nods thoughtfully, 'yeah?'

Jacob went on, 'he felt strongly that you will need a friend in the Engineering Department. So I came to be....'

'Wait a minute,' Richard cut in. 'I didn't tell him I need a friend.'

'I didn't say he said you said that. He just told me you'll need a friend.'

Richard frowned at him. 'I don't know what you guys are up to. Whatever it is, I don't quite understand. I will appreciate it if you leave me ....'

'It's okay,' Jacob said apologetically. 'I'll go away if you consider me a nuisance but I want you to know that we mean well for you. Members of the Christian Campus Fellowship always help new students get acquainted with the school environment. If you could spare me few minutes to share some things with you, I will be glad.'

Richard hesitated for a while before he shrugged. He gestures him to sit on his reading chair and said, 'you can be my guest for today but you have to make it snappy.'

Jacob who was naturally pleasant looking gave him smiles that indicated that he was pleased at the invitation. He said, 'thank you.'

He went to sit on the chair while Richard sits on the bed.

'I'm all ears,' Richard told him.

Jacob said, 'like I said, Christians on campus have the duty to tell as many new students as we come across the ills and the goods in this campus. We also have the duty to share with you the gospel, the truth of all ages which can help you sail through the ocean of insanity you'll likely come across here.'

'What do you mean by ocean of insanity?' Richard asked with puzzled expressions on his face.

Jacob smiled. 'You may think that's a figure of speech but it is not. It's a reality… The truth is: we have so many bad guys than good ones on this campus. Here, everybody seeks to influence and outdo others.'

Richard looked thoughtful. 'That is interesting.'

'We have close to thirty different secret cults on this campus alone and all are seeking to recruits members,' Jacob continued. 'More often than not, their focus is always on new students… and for this singular reason we also have stepped up our evangelistic efforts to reach out to as many students as possible before these cult guys reach out to them.'

'I really don't know why you're telling me this,' Richard said, looking somewhat indifferent. 'Obviously, I'm not as vulnerable as you

36

people think and no one can possibly compel me to join any secret cult.'

Jacob smiled, looking patiently at him. He could see that Richard was either ignorant or foolishly overconfident to think like that. 'My brother,' he said, 'anybody can be compelled to join them once they have their eyes set on you… and that's the hideous truth.'

Richard snorted with amusement and curiosity. 'How?'

'Sometimes they come as friends, sometimes they approach you directly and ask you to be member of their cults. And one strong trait about them is that these guys don't take "no" for an answer. They are so ruthless that they can eliminate you if you bluntly turn them down.'

Richard looked irritated, which indicated that he did not believe him. 'That's to say everybody on campus is a member of at least a secret cult, isn't it?'

Jacob replied, 'the answer to that leads us to the good news I want to share with you. There are many Christian Fellowships on this campus as well. The immunity against the menace of the cult guys is to be strong in your relationship with God. Once you're identified with one of the Christian Fellowships on campus, these secret cults would not border you so much. According to our experience with them, once you are a member of Campus Christian Fellowship, our group will surely fend for you and see to it with prayers and sharing the word of God that your stay on campus is peaceful.'

'Are you saying if I'm not a religious person, I'll be a member of a secret cult?' Richard asked immediately.

Jacob smiled, thinking he must be a very smart guy. Somehow smart guys were the ones that were most vulnerable to cultism and often difficult for Christians to convince. He said after a brief hesitation that gave Richard the impressions that he has come to cajole him to be a member of his Christian Fellowship. 'Not really. But the reality is close to that… My brother, what I'm saying is that you cannot afford to be on your own in this campus. If you don't make friends with good people, the bad guys would make you their friend willy-nilly… if you don't stand for something good, you are most vulnerable to fall for anything evil.'

Richard said, 'it looks to me as if you guys are trained to say the same thing. Lekan told me similar thing.'

'Whatever he told you is the truth. I'm simply confirming it. Like I said, it's all in your own interest.'

'I heard all you said,' Richard said, thinking he has spent enough time with him. 'But I don't agree with you that I cannot be on my own. I can. I'm here for my studies and nothing more. If I need a friend I can always make one anytime I like.'

Jacob shrugged. Although he was not giving up, he stood up, ready to leave him for now. 'Okay. Since you don't have anything against friendship, can we at least be friends even if you're not ready to be a member of any of the Christian Fellowships on campus?'

Richard looked reluctant. 'Maybe I....'

'You're not going to turn down my offer of friendship as well, are you?'

There was silence between them.

'It may turn out to be of mutual benefits,' Jacob said with persuading smiles.

Richard returned the smiles. 'You're peculiar guy - almost hard to turn down without having problems with my conscience.'

Jacob burst out laughing with joy. 'That means yes!'

'Yeah....' Richard replied. 'But don't think of dragging me to your Fellowship because you won't succeed with that.'

'If I can succeed making you my friend, what makes you think I can't drag you to the Fellowship with me?'

'You'll need a machine gun to threaten my life before you can succeed.'

Jacob laughed more loudly. 'What! You think I'm that horrible?' he asked, swaying with laughter. 'I have a far better method. I'll pray for you. You'll willingly walk to the Fellowship meeting place without anybody dragging you there.'

'Okay. We'll see then!' Richard said, feeling very comfortable with him. He stood up to see off.

Jacob stretched out his hand at him.

Richard grabbed it and embraced him, saying, 'thank God my first friend on the campus is a godly guy with lots of guts.'

'And thank God my new friend is an intelligent and stubborn guy that can easily be broken,' Jacob replied, giving him a light punch on the chest.

'Oh, yeah?'

*   *   *   *   *

Richard had barely spent six weeks on campus when he came

across Sjay. He was reading one of his text books in an area that was a little far from some rowdy students in his department that have nothing to do except to chat and walk around.

The place Richard selected to do a personal study that day was ideal for reading and at the same time a perfect place for students who were involved in illegal dealings or antisocial acts.

Sjay just finished the small amount of dope he has and he felt like taking more. He looked round for his friends or any guy he could manipulate or force to give him some money to buy some. No one seemed to be around. So he headed for one of the favorite places he always met them. There was no one except the guy that looked like J. J. C. Most of the students in that category that were always busy reading as if their lives depended on it.

He went straight to meet Richard who concentrated on his book. 'Hi, my guy,' he greeted him, looking friendly.

Richard looked at him briefly. He did not seem to like his appearance at all. He looked very untidy, appearing as if he needed to clean up. He wore dirty jean trousers and a shabby jacket. His has rather rough face and unkempt hair.

The contempt way Richard regarded Sjay made it obvious to him that he did not recognize the common features of hooligans, ruffians and secret cult members. The signs were all over him yet this fresh guy failed to see them. He expected him to hurriedly get out of the place if he knew who has come to meet him.

'Hi,' Richard replied after indicating it to him that he was not welcomed. He continued with his studies.

'I feel like taking some coke, man,' Sjay said, trying to introduce himself and hoping to use that as a threat to get whatever he could get from him. 'You've got some cash or coke?'

Richard still did not suspect that he was facing a member of the much talked about secret cult. He looked irritated though he was not looking at him. He replied, 'no.'

Sjay gave him an indulgent smile and asked, 'do you know how I can get some coke?'

Richard was fast losing his patience with him, 'what's your problem, man? If you need some coke, you'll find it at the cafeteria.'

Sjay laughed, thinking he must be a very raw guy. 'I don't mean that kind of coke, silly! I mean cocaine.'

Richard was now angry at him, making him to sound so provoked. 'Do I look like a cocaine dealer to you?'

'Hay, take it easy, my guy. What's up?'

Richard could no longer control his temper even though he tried. 'Give peace a chance and get the hell get out of here!'

Sjay looked a little surprised though he did not have to. It was typical of J. J. C to act foolishly or out of ignorance of whom they were dealing with. 'What?' He asked, 'what did you say, man?'

Richard glared at him, 'you heard me. Keep moving.'

Sjay looked puzzled, probably because he was yet to meet someone so bold or stupid.

'I say move it! Vamoose! Which of it you don't understand? They all mean: get lost!'

Sjay looked as if he was not sure he was talking to him.

'I say go away! You're not deaf, are you? If you are, see this...' He waved at him to leave. 'You can see that, can't you?'

Sjay seemed to recover from what seemed like a shock. He said, 'let ask me you this little punk! Do you know who you're messing around with?'

Richard stood up to face him. 'Who's little punk here? Who the hell do you think you are anyway?'

Sjay moved closer to him and snarled at him, 'you want to chat with me? Before you do, get this into your empty head.' He pointed at Richard's head. '...we own and rule this campus.'

Richard became so furious that he pushed him on the chest.

Sjay pushed him back and bellowed, 'God damn you, man!'

'God damn you and your entire family!' Richard replied in the same violent manner.

'My family?'

Suddenly they began to fight. Richard lifted him up and slammed him on the ground, squeezing his neck.

Around then, Jacob who just finished with a lecture felt the need to look round for any of the students he had been trying to persuade to come to the Fellowship. Although most of them promised to attend one of the services but so far only few had responded. Richard who seemed to enjoy his company was one of them though he was still adamant about not mixing with any group of students. He had been trying to press him in a subtle and friendly way to joon campus Christian Fellowship but he was yet to succeed making him a devoted Christian. With what he noticed about him, he was almost sure that if he did not get him first to the Fellowship, his attitude would attract cult members to make him their member. So he always tried to hang around him each time he was free, engaging him in discussion about God or his academics.

He went to look for him round the lecture room. He was told he was around other lecture halls. He was still looking for him when saw him fighting with someone from a distance. He hurried to separate them.

When he got close to them, he screamed at Richard who was on top of Sjay, 'stop it, Richard!' He pulled him away from Sjay who stood up at once, struggling to maintain his balance. He angrily pointed at Richard and spat out under his breath, 'you! You just dug your own grave, man. I'll see to it that you rot there.' He began to go away.

Richard tried to follow him but Jacob held him back. He cried at him, 'wait and let's finish this once and for all if you're so tough.'

Sjay looked back and replied breathlessly, 'we'll continue the fight soon enough, you living dead!'

'Who is a living dead?' Richard asked. 'You're the zombie.'

Jacob held him in both hands, looking more impatient. 'I say stop it, Richard! Are you out of your mind?'

Richard pulled away his hands from him. 'Leave me alone!' He went to sit down again.

Jacob stood in front of him. He asked, 'do you have any idea of what you just did?'

'The guy tried my patience by calling me names,' Richard replied.

'Is that why you had a fight with him?'

'I can do without any of your judgmental attitudes. So leave me alone!'

'I take it that you don't know who the guy is.'

'I don't care who he is. He's a crazy guy for all I know and I had just proved it to him that every normal person has an average level of insanity in him.'

'That's very philosophical but we'll see if you'll survive the mess you just created for yourself.'

Richard looked at him. 'And what does that mean?'

Jacob shook his head silently. 'That guy is a member of one of the ruthless cults on this campus.'

Richard snorted. 'And so what?'

'You can expect trouble any moment from now… and that's what he's trying to tell you.'

He looked indifferent as he said, 'I've lived in this world long enough to know that everybody is troubled. So I'm prepared for trouble.'

Jacob shook his head again, 'my friend, life is more complicated than that… Right now, you just declare a battle with cult guys. There's nothing you or I can do to help this situation except to pray.'

Richard looks indifferent.

Jacob shrugged and left. He knew only time would tell if he would be a member of The Black Skulls or opt out of school.

CHAPTER FIVE

The members of the Black skulls were having the usual meeting where they gave reports on steps they have taken so far about having new members.

The Capo sat on his high chair as usual, listening to the progress reports from some members. So far, they have six students to recruit even though the target was about twenty. Because there were other cults with similar aim or target. Apart from these, there were other groups on campus like the Christian fellowships, Muslim society, social clubs and pressure groups who were also seeking to influence the students to become their members. Getting people to join any group of students had turned into intense competitions withon campus. So, to a large extent, having six students to initiate into the cult within at short time was appreciable if not so impressive. Even then, going by what the cult required, those six fresh students were the most qualified among others. Four of the qualified students were not new in secret cults. They have been operating as cult leaders since they were in Junior secondary schools, years before they came into the University. The other two students were just violent guys. It was a lot easy for the Black skull members who came in contact with them to fish them out through their traits.

After the report, the Capo told them he was not satisfied with their efforts so far though he encouraged them to put more efforts. After the presentations of reports, everyone was told to present their requests. This was usually the time complaints about fellow students or lecturers were made. The cult would decide what to do on the spot.

Sjay presented the case of the guy called Richard Moore, a fresh student in the engineering department, living at Inner Temple. Of course, he knew he had to present the detailed information about his victim if he really wanted the cult to do something about it.

He told the cult how they had a fight, how he took advantage of his state of stupor that was caused by the drugs he had taken that day

43

and how he disgraced him. 'The guy,' Sjay continued, 'obviously doesn't know me… He's new on campus and he thinks he's tough. I believe that's the reason he molested me. He thinks he can go away with it.'

Capo waved at him to keep quiet.

He became silent at once.

'Sjay, you're blabbering!' Capo said expressionlessly. 'Nobody can hear you. Do you hear yourself?' There was silence. 'If you can hear yourself, tell us what you're trying to say.'

Sjay knew that was a sigh that the Capo was mad at him. So he kept quiet.

'Answer me!' He roared at him.

Sjay fell at his feet. 'I'm sorry, Capo.'

The Capo shook his head slowly and snarled, 'you're a disgrace to brotherhood. A punk beat you up....'

Sjay said, 'I was high with coke and the guy seems so tough. He's simply too fast for me … really he got what it takes to be a Black Skull…'

Capo sighed and looked round at the rest, waving impatiently. He stood up slowly. 'The only reason I'm going to spare you is because you're not a warrior. If not, I'll have you beaten to the extent that no hospital would be able to bring you back to shape. You know you're not even a fighter yet you went about fighting a punk. You're a weakling.' He looked at him suddenly. 'Next time, don't bring a report like this here. If you meet a guy who doesn't see the traits of The Black Skull in you, don't ever attack him if you don't have a warrior around you. If you attack him and he beats you up as you're trying to make us understand, I'm going to slice your throat into pieces. Do you understand me?'

'Yes, Capo,' Sjay said, nodding vigorously.

The Capo looked at rest and said in a loud voice, 'Black Skulls!'

The rest chorused, 'brotherhood is life but the flesh, the blood and the bones of others are nothing!'

Capo said, 'the guy that failed to see the logo of The Black Skulls in our member shall be taught a lesson… not because we want to take revenge… No… but to plant terrors on others who might dare to lay hands on any member of this great cult…'

The rest responded, 'The Black Skull.'

The Capo looked at Sjay, 'you deserved the beatings you received from this punk but the shame is what the brotherhood will not tolerate.' He paused for a while before he asked, 'I supposed you have

44

enough information on how you can lead our guys to him, don't you?'

'Yes, Capo,' Sjay replied.

He pointed at three men and said, 'you, you and you - the three of you shall join him and bring the punk down here right now. I don't care what it will cost you to accomplish the task. I want to see this punk right now… take the operation car and the weapon that will aid your operation and get the job done. This punk has a strong case to answer this noble sitting.'

Sjay and the three men stood up, bowed before Capo and left the place.

*   *   *   *   *

Richard was deep asleep in his room after reading till it was almost midnight. He really could not afford not to study so hard since a lot of things depended on it. His mother and siblings were counting on him to lead the family out of the state of constant needs into state of abundance. He wanted to become a civil engineer and help his siblings to become university graduates too. Really, his mother had gone through so much despite all his father has achieved to make the family comfortable. Hence, he was constantly reading to the extent that he soon became addicted to his studies. If he did not read for a day for whatever reason, it would seem as if he has lost so much.

Jacob had met him again the day after his encounter with the cult guy and reminded him that he was in a deep shit and only God could get him out. All he had said never made sense to him. Surely, no man could duel with him for he was always prepared for trouble. Of course, just as Jacob try to warn him, he soon realized that by dealing with a cult guy, he was actually dealing with a monstrous cult that was ruthless and deadly enough to eliminate him.

Some violent looking guys burst into his room round 2 a.m, about two hours after he had gone to bed. The door of his room, however solid it was, could not prevent them from bursting inside. He jerked up from the sleep when he heard their noise, looking round with confusion. He wondered what was happening in the dark environment. Soon one of the guys switched on the light after they gained access into the room. There and then, he saw the cult guy he had fought with few days ago. He came with his friends, looking murderously at him.

45

'Hello, tough guy!' Sjay said with a wicked grin across his face.

Richard sensed danger at once. He made the frantic effort to escape from them by hitting the man by the door, hoping to break through the three men that stood by the door. He underestimated their strengths but, at least, he had to try and break away. One of them pushed backward with a karate kick on his chest.

Richard fell backward and stood up again almost immediately. He paused for a while, still thinking of how to escape from them.

'You really believe you're so tough, don't you?' Sjay said.

'What do you want from me?' Richard asked in a gruff voice.

'We want you at the court of The Black Skulls,' Sjay told him while the rest silently studied Richard's movements.

'Why?'

Sjay was the only one that laughed. 'You're asking me, tough guy?'

'Haven't I got the right to ask?' Richard asked. He was actually thinking of how to deal with men at the door.

'We just want to see how tough you are.'

Richard suddenly made another attempt to break through the men at the entrance in order to escape but the rest grasped him and hit him on the head. He screamed with pain and fell down unconsciously.

One of the men say, 'he seems tough alright.'

'We'll see how tough he is,' the second guy replied.

'Let's go, guys,' Sjay said.

They dragged Richard out of the room.

Richard woke up as the men took him to their meeting place in a car. Some minutes later, he found himself face to face with the campus deadly vice ring which he had heard so much about. He did not need to be told how brutal and evil the cult guys must be. For reason which he could not explain, he was not afraid of them. He saw them as human beings who thought they were superior to others because they were violent. The leader who was sitting on a high chair did not look like someone who could defeat him easily if they were to have a fight, one on one.

Capo and most of the members of the cult could see that he was not afraid of them. Unlike most of the people that were brought to face them as their victims in the past, he looked tough, giving some of them the impression that he also belonged to a violent cult. Although, being a fresh student, they knew he was not likely to be a member of a cult on campus yet they could not help wondering what gave him so

46

much courage to stand before them without feeling uncomfortable.

'I was told you're a fresh guy,' Capo said calmly. 'Are you a fresh man?'

'Why should I answer your question, man?' Richard asked with complete contempt.

Moduola, one of the special guards of the Capo made an attempt to hit him on the face but Capo stopped him with a wave of his hand.

Moduola looked angrier as he stepped backward.

'Are you a member of a cult on this campus?' Capo asked with the same calm expression.

'What if I am or I am not?' Richard said harshly.

'We know you're not,' Capo said. 'If you're, we'll have known. You're just a common rascal.'

'And who are you, guys?' Richard asked, looking round at the cult members around him.

Capo laughed. He was really enjoying himself. 'We don't have to introduce ourselves to you. You just go round the campus and tell other students that you had an encounter with the Black skulls. Their reactions will tell you who we are.'

Richard snorted. 'I know who you guys are.'

'Do you?' Capo shot a glace at him. 'You know who we are and yet you have the guts to challenge and embarrass one of us?'

'If one of you is as weak as that, it shows you guys are not as strong as you think. You only think you're strong because you deal with an individual as a group. If you guys want to prove your strengths, why not deal with me as a man to a man.' He waved round at the men. 'See, it takes four guys to get me here. If you had sent only one person to bring me down, I won't be here. That's to prove to you you're not as strong as you think.'

Capo roared again with laughter even though none of the cult members found it funny. They were really angry and anxious to know what would come out of the insults they have to endure. 'You see, my guy,' he said after a while, standing to pace round him, 'you've been dealing with a weakling, not a warrior.'

'That's not an excuse, buddy,' he told him frankly.

Capo continued to smile, nodding with understanding. 'I like your guts, my guy, but let me ask you: what makes you think you can deal with each of us?'

'I have what it takes! What makes you strong, as I said, is the number of you. Even then I'm not afraid of you. Williams Shakespeare said that cowards die many times before their deaths but the valiant

47

never taste death but once.'

Capo walked slowly and thoughtfully, still smiling. He looked at the rest and said, 'you know what I like about this guy? He's very brave and confident. He looks strong, tough and smart. The very things we need in our warriors.'

'Save your breath, cult guy,' Richard snapped. 'If you think I'm going to be one of you, you're missing the point.'

'You're not to decide if you will be one of us or not,' Capo told him. 'I am to decide that.'

'What makes you think you can decide what I'm to do?'

'The reason is because I'm in charge here,' he told him, smiling at him with amusement. 'I can see that you're talking out of overconfidence or sheer ignorance. In fact, I like to believe you're more of a dare devil than a big fool.'

'And what does that mean?'

Capo went to pat him on the shoulder in a friendly manner. 'You're either going to be one of our warriors in this brotherhood or you're a dead man.'

'I'll rather be a dead man,' Richard replied firmly.

'Why do you want to die when you have the chance to live and enjoy all kinds of things we are ready to offer you?'

'What have you got to offer?' Richard asked. He added almost immediately, 'I don't expect a reasonable answer anyway because you've got nothing good to offer.'

Capo smiled again. He was more amused than angry. So he said in a cool voice, 'we've got money, women, prestige, connections to offer you - name whatever you want, we'll get it for you.' He snapped his hand. 'With just a snap - just like that.'

'Now you trying to persuade me, aren't you?'

'Nop! I'm just having a friendly chat with you because you're already one of us even though you don't know it yet.'

'I make the decision whether to join you or not. You are not to do that.'

'You don't seem to know your position here, do you?' Capo asked. 'You're our prey and I decide what to do with you.'

'You must have considered yourself God then,' Richard told him firmly. 'The good thing here is that you're not - not even close to anything called a god with small g.' He waved indifferently round the men again. 'You're all bunch of em.... What can I say? Bunch of hooligans.'

All the men except Capo looked provoked. They expected him to give them instruction to teach him one or two lessons for insulting them.

Capo sensed their feelings. He smiled as he addressed them, 'Guys! I see this cheap punk as one of us. He's an ignorant member. Let's treat me like that. We'll resolve to speak the language of violence if he does not understand the language of brotherhood.' He walked round Richard as if he was thinking of what to do with him. 'You said you can deal with each of us one on one?'

'Yes! What makes you stronger than me is the number of guys here....'

'One of your problems is: you talk too much,' Capo snapped. 'I expect simple yes or no. We don't need a lecture here, man.' He paused, looking at him straight in the eyes. 'Because I like to honour a guy with courage like you, I have a proposal for you.'

'I'm not interested,' Richard replied quickly.

'I'm afraid you have no choice but to listen to me unless you want me to force you...' He looked round the cult members. 'Black Skulls warriors can stand on their feet.' When most of the men stood up, he faced Richard and said, 'I want you to choose a guy you think you can defeat among these guys. If you're able to beat him, I promise to let you go and nobody will border you. But if he beats you, you're going to be initiated here tomorrow as a member of the Black Skulls... That's the best deal you can get under the circumstances here.' He looked deep into Richard's face. 'Do we have a deal?'

Richard replied in a firm voice, 'yes.' He looked round at the men and finally pointed at one of them, whose appearance was deceptive. Although the guy did not look weak or strong, he was actually one of the toughest guys to defeat in any combat.

The guy jumped up with joy.

Capo clapped his hands excitedly and went back to take his seat. He said, 'show time! As a way of introduction, your choice of opponent is called Slippery Demon! I can see you think he is an easy prey... but you have not noticed that he is truly mad with you for your insults and insubordination.' He looked at Slippery Demon, 'be easy on the guy, Black Skull. I know he is no match for you. You can have with him the chat which we normally have with those who need to be taught one or two lessons but don't crush him.'

Slippery Demon bowed before Capo and answered, 'as your lordship pleases...' He faced Richard and gave him an indulgent smile. 'Let's chat, my guy!'

Richard warmed up, boxing the air like a boxer. He seemed

49

ready to aim and hit a sensitive part of his face.

Capo smiled, looking amused. 'Be careful, man.' He looked at other members. 'Our guy is so sure of himself … But yo, men, he is more of an amateur boxer to me than a cheap punk.'

'There's no cause for alarm, Capo,' Slippery said.

Richard suddenly rushed to hit him on the face, hoping to take him by surprise but Slippery was ready for him. He received the punch with his forehead that felt like a cold and solid steel.

Richard looked as if he felt a sharp pain on his hand. As Slippery moved towards him, he tried to hit him again with the other hand. He caught it and tried to wring it by pulling it sideways. Richard wrinkled his face with pains though he made no sound. Having hurt the right hand, he could not use the left to free himself.

Capo said, 'I told you not to crush him. He's not a victim.'

Slippery hit Richard on the neck. He passed out and fell down on the ground.

Capo looked disappointed. 'This fight is too brief for me to enjoy. This is not the show I expected from a guy who seemed so confident in himself. He's not even as tough as I thought.' He looked at Sjay. 'You and the rest can take him back to his room. Get all the items we will need for his initiation ready. He'll be initiated here tomorrow.'

The men stood up to lift Richard up from the ground. A moment later, they took him away.

Richard did not wake up until Jacob came to check him in the afternoon in room. He was just coming from the lecture that day when he looked for Richard where he was supposed to be having lectures too. When he was told he did not show up, he wondered what was wrong. It was quiet unusual for him to miss any lecture. He was so dedicated to his studies that nothing could distract him. During the break between the second and third lectures, he decided to dash down to see him in the room. As usual, there were few people around as most of the students that lived in the house have gone for lectures. He met one of his neighbours who was also student on the way and asked if Richard was around.

'Yes, I guess so,' the student told him.

'Why didn't he go for lectures?' Jacob asked involuntarily.

'When you see him in his room, you can ask him but I guess he's having problem with some… I guess it's not my business.'

Jacob wore concerned expression as he asked, 'he's having problem with who?'

'When you see him, ask him what's wrong. If he wants to tell you, he'll tell you,' the student started walking away while he paused to think. The student paused for a while and said, before he finally getting out of the building, 'the guy attracted some problems here in the middle of the night. So watch out for him.'

Jacob did not really look surprised. He said, 'thanks.'

CHAPTER SIX

The door to Richard's room was not locked when Jacob got to the place. In fact it was slightly opened. He pushed it and went inside. He knew it at once what must have gone wrong with Richard. What he expected must have happened. What he needed to find out now was if he had been initiated into the cult or not. If he has, there was little or nothing he could do to help him. After all, he had warned him and his blood was cleared off his neck. If he had not been initiated, that would be a miracle. Whatever the case, he knew Richard needed God's intervention before he could be rescued from the cult guys.

He had to tap Richard several times before he woke up. When he did, he robbed his neck with both hands as if he could feel some pains. He leaned backward on his bed and looked at Jacob drowsily. 'Hi, Jacob....'

'Hello, Richard.'

'What happened to me?'

'I should be asking you that,' Jacob said. 'Are you ill?'

'No...' he said slowly, recalling the event that led him into unconsciousness, making him to look confused.

'I didn't see you at the Department ... does that mean you don't have a lecture today?'

Still feeling uncomfortable, Richard replied, 'I...don't know. What's the time?'

'It's past noon. By my calculation you've missed two lectures already.'

Richard sat up on the bed, leaning on his back with a pillow.

'You must have good reasons for missing two lectures at a go,' Jacob said, looking concerned.

'I'm seriously wounded...' He stood up unsteadily. Jacob went to support him and gently made him lie down on the bed, sitting down beside him.

Richard muttered, 'the bastard,' before he said to him, 'thanks.'

'You're welcomed.' There was a brief paused before he said, 'Richard, why not tell me what's wrong with you?'

He looked very reluctant. 'It's….nothing so…so serious really.'

'You expect me to believe me that? I know something is wrong. One of your neighbours told me you attracted problem into the house in the mid night.' He paused again before he asked, 'The Black Skulls were here?'

Richard frowned at him. 'How do you know that?'

'Remember I told you to expect problem, didn't I?'

Richard moaned with both pain and regrets. 'Yeah.'

He stared at him steadily and asked, 'have you been initiated?'

'Of course not,' he replied and then narrated what happened to him. He concluded the story by saying, 'to be sincere with you, I don't know how I got back to my room but after I was knocked out, I heard the leader telling some guys to get ready some items that'll be used for my initiation tomorrow.'

Jacob looked puzzled, 'you had a fight with one of them? What's wrong with you? I told you those guys are ruthless.'

'I was sure I can handle this guy but I was wrong. The guy is much stronger than I estimated… In fact I didn't know I was in deep shit until I got in.'

'Do you know your escape from them without getting initiated is a miracle?'

'You think so?' Richard asked. It was his turn to looked puzzled. If it was a miracle, then God must be on his side.

'I know so…This is a miracle,' Jacob replied quickly. 'Going by what we know about these guys, you're supposed to be dead or initiated when you were in their midst.'

'Really?'

'Yes….'

'But the fight is not over yet.'

'Yes, I know so …'

'The leader told me if I'm able to beat Slippery Demon guy, he'll let me go but if he defeats me, I'll be initiated tonight.'

'Your boldness must have actually led to the bargain you got from him.'

'You're right. He said something like that but Slippery Demon beat the hell out of me… I was knocked out in no time. He could have crushed all the bones in my hand if the leader had not stopped him.'

'Do you notice that the devil used your weaknesses against you?' Jacob asked after a brief silence, thinking of how to let him see his predicament.

'How do you mean?'

'Your temper and stubbornness are something you need to work on… Each of them is a terrible weakness, you know.'

'You think I'm stubborn and hot tempered?'

'Yes. These weaknesses are deemed to be strengths of most cult guys. That's what they look for before they come after you. They worked against you as you can see them now.'

Richard looked thoughtful as he recalled what his mother told him one mid night shortly before resuming to school. 'Could this be the reason my mum wants me to do a part-time course instead of coming here?'

'Really?'

He nodded and then told him what she said about campus life and what she feared. 'I promised her I'll not join the bad wagon.'

'Poor mother,' Jacob said as if talking to himself. 'You have broken the promise that means a lot to your mum.'

'But I have no intention of doing that!'

'Remember I also warned you, didn't I?' Jacob asked him gently. 'Can you imagine how she'll feel if she gets to know what is happening now?'

'Yeah. I am a damn fool not to believe what I am up against,' he said. He added almost immediately. 'Don't get me wrong. I'm not giving up. No matter what they do, I'll rather die than to be one of them. The guys are mean and evil.'

'Instead dying, why not leave this campus today. In fact this very moment…'

'Of course, I'm not going to do that,' he snapped. 'Why should I leave the campus for them? I'm going to deal with each and every one of them.'

'How are you going to do that?' Jacob asked, strangely amused. He wondered when he would learn his lesson.

'I'm yet to figure it out.'

'My friend, don't fool yourself again. It's your weakness that got you into this mess in the first place. The same act can cost you your life if you don't do what I tell you to do.'

'No.'

Jacob thought of the best way to educate him about the implication of his encounter with the Black Skulls. His voice softened as he said, 'think of your poor mother back at home, thinking of his son becoming a civil engineer. She would be heartbroken if you walk into the death trap. I don't want you to die like a chicken.'

Richard waved at him indifferently, looking thoughtful. Somehow, he still believed there must be a way to tackle the cult guys without having to run from them. 'What do you expect me to do now? Surrender?' He shook his head stubbornly. 'Not when I still have my last breath. Nobody wins a battle by running.'

'Remember he that fights and runs away lives to fight another day... Of course, I'm not asking you to surrender. The question is: can you stand up against them alone?'

'That's a point... but one needs to do something. We can't continue to have people like that terrorizing the students on this campus or initiating them into their cults even against their wills. One thing I am sure of is that you empower these devils when you fear them. More so, if you fear being attacked, you're already under attack - by fear.'

'You have not answered my question. Can you tackle them alone? It takes an army to tackle an army. Any soldier that tries to fight an army is only dicing with his life, no matter how good he is. If you experience the way these guys kill one another, you'll be shocked. Last year, there was a conflict between two different cults and so many students lost their lives. You may wonder what caused the conflict. It was a girl. Can you believe that?'

'Still, that does not justify me to leave the campus because of them.'

'You must consider this as a divine directive and decide to become a member of the Campus Christian Fellowship. I believe Jesus will protect you if you're one of us.'

'There you go again.... Are you saying Jesus will come down and fight those guys?' He stood up from the bed. This time he seemed to have recovered his strength. 'Let's face it squarely. You make me feel that you're afraid of them. Someone needs to stand up and face these guys.'

'Why are you so ignorant and naïve, Richard?' Jacob suddenly lost his impatience with him. 'This is a problem the government finds difficult to handle. You... an individual person wants to handle it. Fine! Go ahead but I have to tell you that they have godfathers among the politicians and top government officials. Do you think all the money spent on acquiring weaponry is from these groups on campus? No! They are sponsored from the outside and that's the reason they feel they can defy the school authority and get away with it. Let me give you another surprise package. Some lecturers are part of them....'

55

Richard suddenly reflected his first encounter with Sjay as he said, '... You want to chat with me? Before you do, get this into your empty head: we own and rule this campus....'

Jacob's voice jerked him back to reality. 'You are up against militant if not military strengths.'

Richard frowned at him.

'Yes, that's what you're up against. I'm not exaggerating their strengths. You want to fight them, go ahead and fight them. It would take a crazy guy like you to challenge them anyway.'

'You make things sound so hopeless,' Richard said with frustration. 'Going by what you say now, it'll be a suicide mission if I don't join them as they want. I don't see how anyone else can help me. If you can't beat them, as people say, does that means I have to join them?'

'I'm not moved by what people say,' Jacob replied. 'I'm moved by the word of God. The word of God says one with God is more than the majority. And if God is with us, who can be against us? God also tells all his children that greater is he that is in us than he that is in the world. If there is any group that can tackle all the cults combined together, it is the Christ's and that is the Christian fellowship on this campus. We've had encounters with them in the pass yet we always defeat them.'

Richard sighed in resignation. 'Jacob, for the first time in my life, I'm going to trust someone with my life. But are you sure I can entrust my life to your group?'

'I don't want you to entrust your life to any man because no man has the power to protect you. Instead, you must give it to Jesus Christ and trust in him for everything, including protection. Okay?'

He nodded. 'Okay.'

'You better clean up and pack your luggage now. You're going home... and before you leave, we have to see the President of the Campus Christian Fellowship first. The President of the S.U.G is a member of our Fellowship. The two presidents can get us the support we need.'

'Is this the only way out - I mean leaving the campus?' Richard asked with confusion.

'Trust me that's the only way out for now,' he replied, 'since you're supposed to be initiated tonight.'

Richard was still reluctant.

'Hurry up!' Jacob said impatiently. 'We've got no time to waste. Besides, the guys could have placed someone to monitor all your activities.'

'Oh, my God,' Richard muttered and started getting ready to leave the campus.

*   *   *   *   *

Sjay and Magol were at the cafeteria, taking soft drinks and snacks.

Magol was one of the warriors in the Black skulls. In fact it was in battles he always proved his relevance in the cult. So he always looked forward to the time of conflicts between the Black skulls and other rival cults.

He had been in secret cults since he was in Senior Secondary Schools in the northern part of Nigeria. He was made one of the pioneers of a cult called The Mafias after a hooligan went to the school under the pretence that he was a football coach. He presented papers that convinced the principal that he had come to train some boys to become footballers. The school authority gave him the chance to pick as many boys as he wanted. While training about thirty-five the boys, he had the opportunity to make friends with those who have what it takes to become secret cult members. Without anyone knowing it, the hooligan had handpicked about twenty boys, trained and initiated them into secret cults in an isolated area. Because he was under the pay roll of some so-called patrons and matrons who were always in need of youths that would be used to do some dirty jobs, the hooligans has more than enough money to turn the boys into the vice ring. It would not take long before various authorities discovered that there were monsters in various secondary schools through chains of certain horrifying events. How they came about the monsters was always a difficult question to answer, let alone to fight it. The vice rings continued to exist in many secondary schools in Nigeria through aids that were always made available by patrons and matrons. They also made money through dirty jobs and illicit contracts that were awarded. In the course of training cultists, all the vice rings were taught to be independent and self sufficient, emphasizing on the need to grow in numbers. So no matter how the authorities try to eradicate them, they would continue to exist and even expand to other schools.

Magol did not need to be invited when he got to the university before he found a cult that could accommodate him in terms of violence.

Magol was not as smart as most of the members in the first group in the cult though he was very reliable. The Black Skulls could always count on him to carry his assignments dutifully. He sometimes tried to influence Capo's decisions but all his suggestions were inclined to make war. A typical example was the idea of using violence to compel students to accept Deji, a top secret member of the Black Skulls as President of the Students Union Government during the election. Deji lost the election outright to Enitan, a member of the Campus Christian Fellowship, through the relentless efforts and campaigns of a rival cult called The Red Eyes who saw themselves as campus soldiers and protectors of students.

Magol pushed his reasons to enthrone Deji by all means but the Capo knew the implications of going into wars with the Red Eyes. Not that he was afraid of the Red Eyes who have huge fans among the students. He simply could not see any good reason to cause a bloody massacre if The Black Skulls went into war with the Red Eyes. So the Capo had rejected his suggestions but the hatred and grudges against the Red Eyes remained unvoiced by anyone. To most of the members of The Black Skulls, The Red Eyes trampled on their pride and dignity to gain popularity among the students. The Capo, however, assured them that they would go into war with The Red Eyes if they overstepped their boundaries.

Magol saw Richard and Jacob walking briskly towards the direction of the lecture hall behind the cafeteria. He tapped Sjay's arm and pointed at them. 'See our guy over there.'

Sjay looked sharply at his direction.

'I wonder where he's going with that guy in such a hurry,' Magol said.

'I guess the guy with him is his friend. He's the one that separated us when we had the fight.'

'And who the hell is the guy?'

'He's fellowship fanatic,' Sjay said. 'I think he must have told him what was about to happen tonight.'

Magol looked at him. 'Are you sure?'

'It's a guess work, man. I'm not sure.'

'I better find out what's happening and report to Capo right away.'

He stood up and followed them, taking his time to watch who or what they were looking for.

CHAPTER SEVEN

Enitan Kolade, the President of the Students Union Government, popularly known as the S.U.G President was with the President of Campus Christians Fellowship, a join group of most of the student fellowships or churches in the school.

Enitan was a born and bred leader. He exhibited the traits since he was in primary school where he was made the head boy. When he got to secondary school, he was made the class captain because of his outstanding academic performance and the way he mobilized his mates to perform class assignments. He was made the head boy in Junior Secondary School where he used his position to establish a Christian Fellowship in the school. He was always found in the company of those who were far ahead of him in academics and experience. He was humble and so intelligent that other students always sought for his advice. He knew how to marshal people towards a good cause without caring who got the credits. Even though some leaders frequently criticized him as a man with manipulative skills yet people listened anytime he wished to address them. His skills in handling people became obvious shortly after he became a medical student.

He was actually admitted to study for a diploma in medical science for two years before he gained admission through direct entry to study medicine. When he was just in two hundred level, the students in the faculty decided to go on rampage and protest against the poor infrastructures and lack of adequate materials for experiments. The students' leaders in the faculty were not diplomatic and skillful in the way they handle the matter. So it was hard for them to control the emotions of the students until Enitan ventured to calm the students down. With the help of the leaders around him, everybody was made to listen to what he has got to say. He made a great impact on them that day by making them to see things through humanitarian perspective.

He said, 'many of us are going to be doctors. Lives and health of people are going to be entrusted into our hands. That means we have the privilege to save lives. We can rightly say we are in humanitarian profession. No mater what you make in the profession, it not worth the lives we are supposed to save. If we are in that kind of profession, we can say we are humanitarians and we are all responsible. If we embark on rampage, we give rooms for people who are not part of us to destroy the little infrastructures which we are complaining about. If that happens, guess who suffers. Who you think will suffer or pay for them?'

'The students,' some of them said in different ways.

'The students are not the only one that will suffer,' he told them. 'Our parents, some of whom struggle to pay our school fees would be the ones.'

'We are not saying we'll destroy thing!' one of the students said.

'You don't seem to get my point, brother,' Enitan had said gently. 'I said those who are not part of us will take the advantage to destroy things. It's happening in other faculties. We can't afford to be labeled irresponsible if that happens. By our profession, we are leaders. We lead by examples.'

'What do you want us to do now?' another student asked. 'We can't let things continue like this.'

'I suggest, just like our leaders are trying to say, we let them tender our complaints to the University authority. If the authority cannot help us, let's ask them if we can send our representatives to the governor with our complaints. If the governor does nothing, we call on stakeholders, including our parents and politicians who want to make names for themselves to come to our aid. It may not be a good options but it's better than going on rampage. If there is no better idea than this, let's go for it.' Though he did not know his suggestions made sense to most of them, he actually said that to stop the students from going on rampage. He had hoped the leaders would have enough time to think of solutions to the problems. By the time Enitan finished talking with them, most of them have calmed down. Some even gave him a round of applause. What made Enitan a hero was the idea of calling on stakeholders in the school. It was stakeholders like some rich parents that actually solved the problem. Since that day, his profile as a leader began to rise, serving in various capacities in the student's union before he became the S. U. G President.

Enitan was from a devoted Christian background. So humility was part of his leadership style. He was a member of the Campus

Christian Fellowship whose other members did all they could to ensure that he was elected the S. U. G. President. If he was not made to believe that he was a leader who must lead all the students on campus, the chains of problems that went along with the position were more that enough to make him resign his appointment. He had to make friends with all sorts of people, including cult and other dreadful guys on the campus just to ensure peace but the more he offered his unsolicited friendship, the more some people looked for reasons to provoke and cause trouble on campus.

Jide Otefisan, the President of the Campus Christian Fellowship was also a leader though not as diplomatic as Enitan. He was an apt learner who read a lot. This often reflected in his communications, especially when sharing the word of God. His constant studies and applications of what he had learnt made him a seasoned leader. Because he had taught the word of God at different places, impacting lots of people, he had occupied a few executive positions at the Joint Campus Fellowships before he became the President the Campus Christian Fellowships.

Jide had a lot of influence on many people, including some lecturers and students union leaders. Whenever Enitan ran into problems while trying to bring together the University authority and the students, Jide and few other fellowship leaders were always around him to encourage and pray with him. In fact, it was largely due to the efforts of the Christian leaders that he was able to defeat all his opponents in S. U. G Presidential election. Fellowship leaders have mobilized the people to pray and even fast so that wrong people would not be made to lead the students. The fellowship members have gone out of their ways to go from one hostel to another to persuade people to give their votes to those who really deserved to lead them. Before long, Enitan had begun to gather more supports than any of his opponents despite their efforts to win the election. When he emerged as the winner, there were protest among the supporters of losers but it was resolved when leaders from various groups on campus, including the Muslims finally accepted Enitan as the winner.

It has never been easy to be a leader in a campus that was notable for student unrest, abuse of powers, conflicts among cultists and even serious crimes.

Enitan was with Jide to seek for advice on how to handle a problem between a female student and a lecturer in her department. She claimed that the lecturer in question failed her in the last examination because she refused his love advances. She requested to have her paper re-marked. At first, her request was turned down until the S. U. G got involved. When the paper was re-marked, there was little difference in the scores. When the matter was eventually made to rest, the student came up again with another claim that the lecturer threatened to fail her again even when she re-sat for the examination. The matter was again brought to Enitan who told her to look for proof that the lecturer actually threatened her. She asked of the way she could go about it. Since he could not think of a way out, he sought for Jide's advice on how to lay the matter to rest.

They were having the discussion about the female student when Jacob brought Richard went to the two Presidents.

Jide smiled at them when they got closer. 'Hi, gentlemen.'

'This must be a presidential discussion... My dear Presidents!' Jacob said cheerfully. 'I believe meeting you together is divine. We're looking for either of you when one of your hall mates told us he saw the two you here.' He gestured at Richard. 'This is my new friend - Richard.'

Jide, still smiling at them, stretched out his hand to Richard who shook it. 'Hello.'

'Hi!'

Jacob looked at Richard, gesturing at Jide. 'He ... is Pastor Jide, the President of Campus Christian Fellowship.' He gestured at Enitan. 'And here is Brother Enitan, the President of the Students' Union Government.'

Enitan delightedly shook hands with Richard. 'How are you, Brother?'

'I'm fine. Thank you.'

'Richard is a new student here,' Jacob continued.

'I see,' Jide said.

'I thought as much,' Enitan said.

'I hope we are not interrupting your presidential discussion. We have a big problem which required presidential solutions.'

'I see.'

'And what could that be?' Enitan asked

Jacob gestured at Richard again before he said, 'he had an encounter with members of The Black Skulls.'

The two Presidents looked puzzled and then exchanged glances.

'How did he encounter The Black skulls?' Enitan asked.

'I have to confess that I was very ignorant if not stupid,' Richard said in a gentle mannered voice.

'Don't judge yourself,' Jide said. 'Just tell us what actually happened.'

Richard hesitated for a while before he said, 'few days ago, a guy came to me while I was reading in a quiet place and asked me to give him some cocaine. He provoked me on purpose and we ended up fighting.'

Jide frowned. 'You had a fight with a cult guy?'

Richard nodded regretfully.

'As a Christian, you shouldn't have allowed what he did to you to degenerate to that level… Tell me sincerely, are you a Christian?'

Richard did not know what to say. He looked at Jacob to speak on his behalf. When Jacob was hesitant, he looked at the other two men who were staring at him. 'I am from a Christian family… If that is what you mean.'

'That's not what he means,' Enitan said.

'What I mean is: are you born-again?' Jide said.

Jacob now decided to speak for him, 'he has just given his life to Christ after I ministered to him.'

Enitan looked at Jide and shrugged. 'That explains why he had a fight with another person.'

'My brother,' Jide said, 'you are very lucky the school authority is not aware of your melodrama or you will be graduating just about now.'

Richard frowned. 'What do you mean?'

Enitan said, 'obviously, you have not read your student codes of conduct given to you during your orientation programs…   Article 10 subsections 1 prohibits students from engaging in physical combat on campus. One of the founding philosophies of this campus is that students are free to disagree on issues but each one is expected to develop sound reasoning channel through which a strong case could be used to support one's point of view in any situation.'

'So anyone who fights is regarded as unworthy member of this citadel of learning… and such a person will face the disciplinary panel,' Jide added.

'After that a rustication or termination of studentship,' Enitan said.

Richard looked surprised. 'Just like that?'

'Just like that,' Jide said.

'How about the guy?' Richard asked.

'The same thing would happen to him,' Enitan replied.

'What happened after the fight?' Jide asked.

'I guess he reported me to other members of his cult. They came to my room around 2 am today and took me to their meeting place where they decided to initiate me into their cult…'

'How come you're not initiated on the spot?' Enitan asked, looking a little surprised.

'My friend, Jacob made me realize it's a miracle.'

'Miracles like that do occur at times,' Jide agreed. 'When do they plan to initiate you?'

'Tonight.'

'Tonight?' Enitan asked.

Richard nodded silently.

Enitan stood up slowly and looked at Jide. 'Not again. I am getting sick of this. So, this time, I want you Brethren to count me out of this. It'll be a favour if you do.'

'Have your seat, Brother,' Jide said.

He shook his head slowly. 'No. I've got a place to go.'

'Are you afraid of them?'

'You know I'm not. I've tackled them with the power of God many times. As a man, I don't want to have anything to do with those cult guys again.'

'You're our leader when it comes to Students' Union but remember I'm your Pastor. As a good leader and a shepherd, you do not abandon your sheep in the field when they are facing danger. I know and I am sure you are not a bad leader. As your Pastor, I'm asking you to sit down. We have to do something about this.'

Enitan sighed and sat down reluctantly.

'God placing us in the positions of authorities on this campus is not a mistake. We are what we are today by the Lord's grace and for divine purposes. Basically, on this campus we are meant to help follow students like him. We can't walk out of his problem and pretend as if we are not in the position to help him. What do you think Jesus would want us to do? Abandon him in the hands of the cult guys? Or what?'

'We are all human, you know,' Enitan said. 'I still remember what we went through the last time we had an issue with these cult guys. It's hard to think of taking another risk.'

'Anything you do in the name of the Lord is not a risk though it is a task. It is our divine responsibility,' Jide said, patting him on the shoulder.

Enitan smiled. 'You Pastors have a way of striking cords.'

'So we are going to help this brother, aren't we?'

'With you involved, it's hard to walk out,' Enitan groaned. It was obvious that the two were bound by mutual love and harmony.

Jide smiled at him before he looked at Richard, pointing at Enitan. 'That's our real brother talking. He will try to persuade the cult guys to leave you alone.'

'You would have to pray that they heed easily this time around since they have taken him to their meeting place,' Enitan reminded Jide with a rueful smile.

Magol at first stood at a distance, looking at them. He tried in vain to get a hint of what they were talking about. Still looking for anything that would prove if Sjay was right about telling the fellowship guys what happened to him, he walked towards them.

'Here comes, one of them,' Jide said.

The rest looked at his direction.

Magol looked cheerful as he went to bow before Enitan. 'The great President of our small country! What's up?'

Enitan smilingly shook his hands. 'How are you, my guy?'

'I'm cool, Mr President.' Magol cheerfully gave Richard a light punch on the chest. 'Hey, my guy, the tough guy! How are you doing, man?'

Richard did not respond.

'I hope our deal still stands? Don't forget our date tonight.' Giving the rest a kudos sign, he left almost immediately.

'He's talking about the initiation tonight, right?' Jide asked Richard.

He nodded.

'There goes the confirmation we are all waiting for,' Enitan said. 'We have a terrible case in our hands. This is a signal that all eyes are on our brother here.'

'You mean the appearance of this guy is an indication that these cult members are watching Richard?' Jacob asked.

'That is the logic,' Enitan replied.

Jide stood up to pat Richard on the shoulder. 'I must confess to you that your life is in great danger on this campus unless you join the cult.'

'That sounds discouraging,' Richard said quietly.

'I don't mean to discourage you, really. The S. U. G President can testify to that. It may take a full blown war to change the condition we are in right now.'

'I don't know about that but I'm convinced that Jesus can protect me from them. All of you are God's servants. So I hope you guys will help me.'

'I believe our Lord Jesus Christ will surely help us out,' Enitan said.

'We've agreed to help you, haven't we?' Jide said. 'We'll do all we can to get you out of the problem but you have to know that without the help of God, there's nothing we can do. So we'll begin to pray for you and expect God to use brother Enitan to help us get you out of this. More importantly, I hope you realize how an uncensored thoughts, actions and reactions can land one into bigger problem.' He looked thoughtful. 'I believe my President and I are held here in order for you to see us together and that, according to our brother Jacob here, is divine.' He looked at Enitan and smiled. 'Do you believe that, brother?'

Enitan robbed his face with his palms thoughtfully. 'Yeah. But this is not going to be easy.'

'Nobody says it would. It is never easy to be the head. People admire the crown. So they make an idol out of it. But it takes the grace of God to live up to expectation as the leader. That's the reason a leader, especially a Christian that is leading all kinds of people must always say to himself: I can do all things through Christ who strengthens me.'

'Wao!' Enitan seemed charged. 'Another solid message from God. The Lord knows I need the passage you have just quoted.'

Jide smiled. 'Thank God for his word.' He looked at Richard. 'First thing first, you must get out of this campus now. You must go home and stay there for at least a week while we sort things out here.'

Richard frowned, thinking Jacob must have been truly guided by God to tell him to leave the campus.

Jide misinterpreted his expression. 'You want to know why?'

Richard shrugged uncertainly.

'I'll tell you why,' Jide said. 'We don't want you to be caught up in the crossfire. If our guys refuse to heed to peaceful dialogue, then there's going to be a tug of war - all because of you. Therefore, my brother, you better get out of this campus before the cult begins to blow the trumpet of war.'

Richard nodded vigorously. 'Okay.'

'Brother Jacob will give you our numbers. You can call any of us to know the state of things from time to time.'

Richard nodded again.

Jide turned to Jacob. 'You can see us later.'

'All right.'

As the two men left, Jide smiled at Enitan who looked thoughtful.

'To be candid,' Enitan said, 'I find the seat of the President of the

S.U.G very hot. I sometimes feel there's a bomb under the seat, ready to go off at any time.'

Jide laughed. 'Don't worry, it won't explode. If it does, we're both sitting on it together. Remember God tells us that the fire will not hurt us if we pass through it.'

He laughed with him. 'I can now see why all the Fellowships on campus had ensured that I am elected the President. Ever since I occupied the position, it's one problem right after another. Imagine one dealing with the good, the bad and the ugly.'

They laughed again.

CHAPTER EIGHT

Magol went to Capo's residence, a somewhat flashy place which was too luxurious place for students. Of course, the place was provided for him by the godfathers. Most of the members of the Black skulls lived in luxuries and in the companies of the most sophisticated girls on or off the campus. They did not need to strive for ladies. They naturally queued to get their attentions. The cult guys, as the students addressed all of those who were involved in one secret cult or the other, have different ways of getting all they needed without sweating for it. They have the money, the connection and the weapons they could use to bring their victims to their kneels.

Six members of the cult were hanging round Capo's residence, guiding the place. There were always guards around the heads of most if not all leaders of secret cults on the campus. The reason had always been to either protect them or to prove the strengths of the cult. The proof of the strengths sometimes became obvious when a cult leader met another leader probably on their way to in a joint. They always prove superiority to each other through what happened in the place. Often times the weaker cult leader gave way for the strong one. The confrontations of two cult leaders usually resulted into conflicts that sometimes have series of effects on campus. As a way of avoiding conflicts that always claimed lives of their members, most the cult leaders avoided open conflict or confrontation. In fact, some of them tried to make peace with one another but the truth was that all the peace talk among secret cult leaders was only talks of the lips. Most of them would readily go into war if there was any reason to. Only the weak ones which were just growing would sincerely talked about peace.

Magol was at Capo's residence to report what he discovered to him. He greeted the men around the place by crossing his arms against his chest. The men did the same. One of them gestured him towards the door, indicating to him that Capo was inside.

Magol nodded and went to knock at the front door three times.

Capo knew it was one of the cult warriors that was by the door, going by the number of times the door was knocked. He replied from the inside, 'come on in, warrior, in brotherhood we stand.'

Magol replied, 'yes, my lord ...in brotherhood we stand.'

Capo was sitting on a couch, holding a small bottle of brandy in one hand and a half smoked of tobacco on the other hand. He looked at him as he bowed before him.

'You come in peace, I suppose, Magol?' he asked in a jovial spirit.

' Yes, my lord ... I,' Magol said slowly, 'I... em... feel I should inform you that I met the guy we are supposed to initiate tonight with the duo of S. U. G's and that Craze Fellowship's Presidents.'

Capo shrugged indifferently. 'And so?'

'I suspect they want to play cards with us, Capo.'

Capo smiled at him and stood up. 'You know nobody has what it takes to play any game with us.' He patted him on the shoulder. 'Meanwhile I want you to keep an eye on the guy or get someone to do that. Whether they like it or not, our guy will be initiated tonight. I can assure you of that.'

Magol bowed and left almost at once to carry out the assignment.

He was on the move to look for Richard at once. With what he has discovered so far, Richard seemed to underrate the Black Skulls. He suspected that he might be difficult to locate when it was time to initiate him. So he felt he should look for him and keep him in view till he was initiated.

Meanwhile, Richard was already finding his way out of the campus as he was advised by the President of the Campus Christian fellowship. He had packed a few things he needed in a bag and made his way to the school bus stop where he would board a taxi that would take him to a commercial car park. From there he would board another vehicle that would take him straight to Ibadan.

There were other students at the bus stop. They were waiting for taxi that would take them to the car park. As soon as one arrived, Richard rushed to enter the taxi before all the seats were occupied. Within few minutes, the taxi had taken off. Just then, Magol who was informed by a student living around Richard's residence that he saw him not quite long with a bag heading towards the bus stop.

Magol instantly came to the conclusion that he was leaving the campus. He hurried to see the possibility of stopping and kidnapping him until the time of the initiation but he was too late to get him. He saw him afar when the taxi arrived, hoping he would not get the chance in the taxi but it seemed he was aware that someone was pursuing him at the back.

Magol managed to hire a bike rider that would take him to the car park in the town but Richard was already out of sight when he got there. Feeling disappointed, he went back to report to Capo.

'The S. U. G President must have told him to leave the campus,' Magol told Capo who was boiling inside, though he did not express it in anyway.

Enitan has overstepped his boundaries, Capo thought with fury. He was really in the mood to go after his life but he could not take that decision yet. He must give himself time to think. He hated to strike and miss. He loved to strike and get away with it. Enitan was not someone he could eliminate without causing uproar on campus. As the President of the S. U. G, he was a central attention. He held the interests of Student Union, the University Authority, the State and the Federal Government. If he has to eliminate him, he has to do it in style. He would use "smoke screen" method which the Blood Skulls often used to eliminate their victims that held people's attentions. The method involved causing mayhem on the campus by engaging other cults in the conflicts. Many students would be killed along with their victims. This would give everybody the impression that all the innocent students, including their targets were just victims of the conflicts, not victims of The Black skulls.

Getting other cults involved in the mayhem was not a problem at all. If no cult felt obliged to protect the S. U. G President, he knew The Red Eyes would. They have been keeping an eye on him since he became the President, knowing fully that The Black Skulls were humiliated when their candidate lost in the S. U. G Presidential election. As both cults were about the only giants on the campus, they have a way of getting information from each other. They did this through bugs, girlfriends of members and even mobile communications. They used the information to make decisions and tackle each other.

Since Capo was sure The Red Eyes would try to protect Enitan, being their candidate that won the election, The Black skulls would need to find reasons to engage them in the conflict that would supposedly claim the lives of many people, including the S. U. G President's. Though he was quite satisfied with the decision he has made, he never desire to share it with anyone. If he did, some members would be anxious to carry it out and even make it obvious that there was a war in embryo. It was better to keep all his thoughts and decisions to himself until it was time to carry them out.

Richard got home that day without preparations to answer his mother's chain of questions.

'What's wrong?' Titi asked. She was puzzled to see him at home. She did not expect him to come home so suddenly like that. She left the cloths she was trying to iron as he went to drop his bag, sitting on the conch.

'It's nothing serious, mum,' he said indifferently. He looked round for his brothers and sister who have gone to church. There was a pastor who just moved to the neighbouring house with his family. He has been going round the place, telling people about Jesus Christ. Titi and the children used to attend the program on Sundays. There was a three-day special prayer program for those were still in schools. The pastor foresaw it in the dream that some students were going to lose their lives through conflicts in the school. So he felt the need to pray for all the students in the country, using the ones in the church as a point of contact to others. 'Where are Tope and Femi?'

'They've gone to Church,' she replied impatiently. 'You answer my question by telling me why you're here when you're supposed to be in school.'

'I said it's nothing serious.'

'You've been expelled?'

'Of course, not!'

'The students are on rampage?'

'Not really.'

'Tell me what on earth is gong on!' she said eagerly.

'I have to come home because of … em… some boys that are planning to cause trouble. I don't want trouble. So I came home.' That was the only way he could relieve her of her anxiety.

She gave a soft sigh of relief and said, 'I want you to go to Church now and join them in prayers.'

Richard did not show any sigh of surprise though he wondered when his family turned into prayerful Christians. 'Can I rest for a while?'

'No. They must have started it an hour ago. So you have to go right away,' she said. 'It's a three day program. I want you be part of the whole days. I believe it's God that brought you here to be part of it.'

'Why do you believe so?' He asked curiously.

'Well,' she replied without hesitating, 'God revealed it to the Pastor that the devil plans to shed blood of so many students though

71

he doesn't know where.'

Richard frowned. For the first time in his life, he was going to believe that God speaks to his people. If the Pastor could perceive through mere dreams what made him left the campus, then God must have truly spoken to him. 'The pastor must be real,' he remarked subconsciously.

'He's real. You know the reason we decided to be members of the church must be genuine,' she replied. 'Perhaps it is what he perceived in the dream that made God brought you home.'

'Yes, yes,' he said quickly. 'I believe so.' He stood up. 'I better go to the church. Where's the place?'

'I'll take you there myself and introduce you to the Pastor,' Titi said and went into the room to change wile Richard went to drop his bag in his room.

* * * * *

Enitan had been pondering over the matter of Richard and the Black skulls for few days now. He did not know how to go about it despite the fact that he knew he had to talk to Banjo, Capo of The Black skulls if he has to resolve the matter amicably. He was dragging his feet in approaching him, not because he was afraid of him but he was not sure of the consequences. If there was anything he was afraid of it was the uprising the situation might turn out to be. Most secret cults on campus were quite unpredictable. No one could say what they might do to get attention or create fear or prove superiority and or convince the people of their monstrosity. Whatever the solution to the problem, silence was definitely not the way to go out about it. He had kept quiet all the while, expecting something that would drag the S. U. G as a body into the case. So far, nothing has happened and that gave him the unpleasant feelings that The Black skull was up to something dreadful. In order to shoot the problem before it came up, he decided to approach Banjo and talked peace with him. He went to him at his residence. He had to wait outside as one of his boys went to tell him he has a visitor.

Capo who was sitting on the couch in the sitting room, reading newspapers was reluctant to grant Enitan audience when he was told he was waiting for him outside. After a thoughtful moment, he decided to let him know a bit of his mind, at least to let him know the kind of shit he was getting himself into. 'Tell him I'll see him in twenty minutes,' he told Moduala, one of the special guards that brought him the message.

Enitan had to wait outside for exactly twenty minutes before Moduola led him to Capo. He was still reading the newspapers when the two men entered.

Capo waved at Moduala who took his bow and left at once. He looked at Enitan indifferently without asking him to sit. Then he and asked, 'what is the problem, young man.'

Enitan knew all the tricks cult guys usually applied to provoke the people they were forced to relate with. So he did not allow his patronizing attitude to offend him. He smiled and said, 'good afternoon, Banjo.'

'Skip the greetings and go straight to the point. What brings you here?'

'Won't you offer me a seat?'

'Why should I offer my enemy my seat?'

'When did we become enemies?'

'Kindly spare me that nonsense and get straight to what brought you here.' Capo's voice was getting high.

Enitan sighed and sat in front of him.

'I didn't ask you to sit down.'

'I've been waiting outside to see you for twenty minutes,' Enitan said with a rueful smile. 'And you won't offer me a seat here? You're kidding me. Even The Vice Chancellor of the University would not treat me like that.'

'You realize you're in my house, Enitan.'

'I came in peace,' he told him. 'Since you see me as your enemy, I wonder how I'm going to appeal to you.'

'You've come to appeal to me about what?'

'It's about Brother Richard.'

'He's one of my boys,' Capo said calmly and confidently. 'Has he done anything wrong?'

'Unless I'm getting things mixed up, he is not one of your boys and he doesn't intend to be.'

'Is that the reason you asked him to leave the campus?'

Enitan suddenly got annoyed at him. He did not know why he has to tolerate his provocative attitude. He looked stern as he told him, 'Banjo, I think I need to remind you that I am the S. U. G President, the number one student and the leader on this campus. By implication, if you are a real student on this campus, I am your leader, not one of

73

your followers. So don't you ever forget that.'

Capo looked provoked. He snarled, 'do you realize that I can order for your execution right now?'

Enitan laughed and looked round. 'Where is the executioner?' He stood, looking at him straight in the eyes. 'You know that's an empty threat - a bluff. You should know better than trying to frighten me.' He began to pace up and down in front of him. 'Look, Banjo, I don't want to make an issue out of my position as the S. U. G president unless you want me to.'

Capo glared at him and said, 'this ego trip of yours is really offensive and self-destructive. It will land you no where but trouble.'

Enitan sighed. He knew it would be hard to use his position to threaten him. He decided to try another method. 'Alright. If you see it that way, let's lay down our weapons and ego and let's talk peace. Peaceful co-existence is one of the philosophies behind the establishment of the Students' Union, which you are a member.'

Capo stood up slowly to face him. 'How do you expect me to make peace with you when you are challenging my authority to recruit and maintain the membership of my group?'

'You know that's not true. Everybody knows that I love peace but if in the cause of looking for peace, you feel I am a threat to your authority, I am sorry for that.'

'Look here, Mr President, there is no compromise on this issue. I don't want you to interfere on this issue. The guy is ours and that is final. If you want to talk about peace here, that is the starting point. You must agree that the guy belongs to us.'

Enitan was thoughtful for a while. Of course, he was not ready to give Richard to him, not after he had gone this far to refuse being initiated into the Black Skulls. 'You know it's wrong to force him to be your member.'

'I didn't force him,' Capo said. 'We had a deal.'

'What was the deal?'

'Why should I tell you if he didn't tell you the deal?'

'He told me what happened,' Enitan said gently. 'And I don't see any deal between him and the Black Skulls.'

'Really?' Capo sounded annoyed.

'Yes,' Enitan said firmly. 'All the guy is trying to do is to escape from you guys.'

Capo snorted. 'You really don't know much the guy you've come to protect, do you?'

'In any case, he doesn't want to have anything to do with you.'

74

'So we should give up on him?' Capo laughed.

'Yes,' Enitan said gently. 'I've come to beg for his head.'

'The moment he stepped into our midst, he's already one of us. Trying to rescue him from us is declaring war against us.'

'Let me ask you then: do you really believe you can make war with my authority on this campus?'

Capo smiled at him. 'You know you're too small to engage me in any battle.'

'Really? You forget that your group is being funded by scanty and unscrupulous people that use you to achieve their illicit ambitions. Shall I give you my profile if that's necessary for you to refresh your memory? Once again, I want you to know that I represent both the students and the University authorities and by extension I represent the government. But you, on the other hand, represent the underworld. So I've got what it takes to crush you and your group without sweat.'

Capo roared with angry laughter. 'I underestimated you?'

'Yes. I can mobilize the students against you. I can declare you and your group as terrorists on this campus.'

'Slow down, Mr. Peacemaker, you know how much I love wars. I love good fight if I can find one. So you can carry out your threat and see who would lose at the end of the day.'

Enitan knew he was not making any progress with the peace talk. He wondered what made Banjo so mean and bloodthirsty. He said as a final appeal, 'I don't want further conflict in my tenure. If two elephants fight, it is the grasses that suffer. I don't want to jeopardize the lives of those I'm supposed to protect. I know you have the connection with the unscrupulous politicians but, like I always advise, don't let people use you against your people. You've got nothing to gain at the end of the day except ...'

Capo interrupted him, 'this meeting is over!'

'Banjo, your parents send you here to become somebody they can be proud of, not the leader of a bloodthirsty cult.'

'I said this meeting is over. You've provoked me long enough! You know that no one would say half of what you said without paying for it.' He pointed at the door. 'Get lost before you feel sorry for yourself!'

Enitan hesitated for a while before he shrugged. 'Okay, I'll go.' When he got to the door, he turned to look at him again and said, 'you're wrong if you think I am a weak leader. Now I realize that you don't talk peace when it is time to do the right thing.'

75

'Should I take that as a compliment or a declaration of war? Mr President, you must be warned. If you don't stay clear of this, you may be dicing with your life. Remember, this is out of your control.'

He snorted. 'You bluff a lot. I guess empty threat is part of the weapon you use to manipulate your people. You can do what you want. I'll do what I have to do,' he said and then left the room.'

CHAPTER NINE

Enitan later went to tell Jide of the unpleasant outcome of his meeting with Banjo. He added after he finished narrating what happened to him, 'the guy seems determined to cause trouble.'

Jide went to get him some cold fruit drinks which he kept in his small refrigerator for visitors like him. He poured some for him in a glass cup and handed it over to him. 'Here, this would cool you down, brother.'

Enitan took it and prayed briefly over it before he drank some of it.

'Often times what we see as problems are really not problems,' Jide said. 'The real problems are the ways we handle them.' He sat down close to him. 'You feel the pressure of the problem, so to say, because you're the President of Students' Union. If you're just a member like me, you wouldn't feel it this much, you know.'

Enitan nodded with understanding. He sipped the drink and said, 'The guy kept provoking me on purpose so that we may not make headway. I'm not sure if I have handled the problem properly.'

'You have, my brother,' Jide said quickly. 'Actually, you can't do better than that under the circumstances. What I think we should do is to let God take over the matter instead of bordering yourself with what is beyond your power to handle. As leaders, what we do most is to pray and meditate on the word of God. The Bible says in the book of Psalms chapter one verse one and two, "blessed is the man that walketh not in the counsel of the ungodly, nor standeth in the way of sinners, nor sitteth in the seat of the scornful. But his delight is in the law of the Lord; and in his law doth he meditate day and night."

'Have you noticed that each time the cult guys breathed fire and brimstone like that, they usually lose their lives. God has a way of protecting those who trust in him.'

'But,' Enitan said thoughtfully, 'according to the word of God in Ezekiel chapter eighteen verse… em….. I think twenty-two or twenty-three where God says that he does not desire the death of a wicked man but to repent and live.'

'You're right,' Jide replied. 'But then, God still has respect for the power of choice he gave to us right from the time he created man. He gave man power to obey or disobey him when he told them not to eat the forbidden fruit. He could have stopped man from eating it by force if he had wanted to but he gave them the choice to obey or disobey him. He still has respect for that power of choice till today. It is the devil that compels man to follow him but God gives us the option to accept or reject him in our lives. The wrong choices which people have made are what get others who are not in Christ into trouble.

'Besides that, my brother, whether we believe it or not, there are children of perdition just as there are children of God. In Philippians chapter three verse eighteen and nineteen, the Bible talks of many who walk as enemies of the cross and whose end is destruction. Such people are children of predictions and ideal tools for the devil to use to destroy others.

'I've always told everybody I met that you can't keep the power of choice by yourself. It's too dangerous for us to keep by ourselves. If we don't hand over that power to Jesus, the devil will take it by force and use it to destroy us. That's the reason people are initiated into secret cults against their wish.'

'One of the reasons I think the people wants to keep the power,' Enitan said in agreement with him, 'is that people want to control everything, including others. They want to play God and even control God.'

'Yes!' Jide said cheerfully. 'That's a sound point. I remember a sister who told me she prayed like this: "God, you said we should command you, concerning the work of my hands. I want you to give me brother - whatever - as my husband!'

Enitan laughed with him.

'It was not hard for me to use the book of James to balance what she knows about God. Even if you pray to God concerning a thing, you can't tell him how to go about it. Some would go as far as telling God what they want and when to get it. It's absurd to think one can control God like that. Just because he has given all his children the privilege to tender their requests does not give them control over God.'

The interaction was endless but it was edifying. By the time Enitan left Jide's place, he was really encouraged to use his position to do the right things.

Enitan sat alone in an empty lecture room few days after the discussion with Capo of The Black Skulls, trying to read. The problems of students and the cults have taken so much of his time that he hardly had time for studies, which was the main reason he was on campus. Although all the while he thought he was alone, at least the two giant cults have their members watching all his steps. All the Campus Christian Fellowship leaders on the campus could do for him was to encourage him with his good works and pray constantly for his protection. Everybody knew that, by the virtue of his position, he was leading both saints and beasts, including what some students called devil incarnates.

Storm Redhead, The Marshal of the Red Eyes entered the lecture room with six sturdy looking guys. Storm was a dark, tall and slim intelligent looking young man with an aura of confidence and firm leadership. The young men with him dressed like gentlemen but Enitan knew there was nothing gentle about them. Although the Red Eyes seemed to have approval of many students, to him, cult guys were bad guys and there was nothing to approve in them. They were all law breakers and murderers. There was no way they could justify any of their actions on and off the campus.

Storm smiled pleasantly at Enitan as the men dispersed round the lecture room. He went to sit right beside him without waiting for an invitation. He knew he would not invite him anyway because he did not seem to approve of anybody that belonged to anything that looked like a cult. He was always forced to tolerate them because he was the S. U. G President. Up till then, he did not seem to know the great role the Red Eyes had played to get him elected as the President. Though this never bordered the Red Eyes yet there was need to let him know what was going on behind him.

'Hello, Mr. President of our great campus,' he said cheerfully. 'How's the day, my President?'

Enitan said indifferently, 'as you can see, I'm trying to study my books.'

Storm thought of him as ignorant guy and ignorance was indeed destructive. If only this guy knew his life was in danger and they have come to tell him the Red Eyes would protect him, he would not snub him like that. 'Yeah, I can see that. I'm not blind.'

'What do you guys want from me?'

'The question is what you need from us,' Storm said. 'We heard that you're having problems with the Black skulls.'

'Who told you that?' Enitan looked a little puzzled.

'Nothing is hidden from the Red Eyes.'

'I've had enough of you, cult guys. Can't you just leave me alone for a moment and let me concentrate on my studies, please?'

'I can see that you have a wrong impression about the Red Eyes apart from the fact that you're ignorant of so many things. We are obliged to educate you as briefly as possible and to let you know how and why we have to operate on this campus.'

There was a brief silence as he reflected the formation of the Red Eyes just as he was told by his predecessor.

The Red Eyes was forced to be organized when secret cults were growing at an alarming rate during the military area in the country. The cults were almost in power as many people, including some teaching and non-teaching staffs were either brutalized or forced to join. There were so many armed cultists on campus that students constantly live in fear of them. So many students left the University without graduating because they could not live with the prevailing horror and bloodshed on campus. Sights of dead bodies on campus became common. It grew worse when the military government was called to intervene. It became obvious that many government officials were members of the outside secret cults that were connected with the ones inside the campus.

One man who later died in the course of fighting the cults mobilized able students and educated them that if they did nothing to check the excesses of the cults, they would all sleep one day and realize that most of them were dead. He told them that they needed an army that would tackle the cults. At the very least, they should operate as secret security service or what the local people called the vigilante group. Many students came together to form the Red Eyes which symbolized anger and vengeance. Some students who were forced to join the notorious cults pulled out to join the Red Eyes, leaking information about them to the new group. The Red Eyes never saw themselves as secret cult but Secret Service Agents. Although, because of the nature of their operations that often times led to killing of other cult members, they were considered one of the most deadly cults on campus. The group did not mind to be libelled as secret cult as long as they were able to curb the excesses of all the dreadful guys on campus. It took years before students could understand that the Red Eyes were actually fighting for the students. Many, including the founder have died in the course of protecting the students. As part of the orientations of the members, each new member was always mandated to take an oath that they would lay down their lives if there was need while fighting for justice. They were so dedicated to the course that a member of the cult was seen as a hero or heroine. It soon became a fashionable thing to be a member of the Red Eyes. Female students always felt secured if their lovers or even friends were members. Thus the popularity of the Red Eyes was a thing other cults hated with passions.

Before the elections of the S. U. G executives, the Red Eyes had the policy of not getting involved on campus politics. They soon realized that some cults always pushed their members to hold key positions that would give them room to operate as they liked without any challenge from either S. U. G or other groups. With the power of the S. U. G in their hands, cult members would make decisions which would be carried out by the S. U. G executives. With the support of the S. U. G, they could cause the deaths of many people and go away with it. The S. U. G would always be there to sweep the matter under the carpet. It was always easy to know if cult guys were in S. U. G or not. During their tenure, there was always oppressions and bloodshed. In the previous year, shortly before Enitan was elected the President, many students lost their lives because the girlfriend of a cult member was snatched by a final year student. Of course, the final year student was among those who lost their lives in the conflict. If the girlfriend of the cult guy had not agreed to continue her relationship with him, she would have lost her life as well.

The oppression the students usually went through compelled the Red Eyes to get involved on campus politics. The first thing Storm Redhead did was to find out a credible candidate and use the popularity of the Red Eyes to give him the backup he needed to be elected. When Enitan emerged the winner of the election The Black Skulls who has Deji, their secret member as their candidate, became silent but it was obvious that the members were seeking for ways to eliminate the new President. Now that he has found a reason to attack, the Red Eyes felt the need to inform Enitan what was going on behind him.

'The Black skulls plan to attack you,' Storm told Enitan after a brief silence, thinking of what he needed to tell him and what he must not know. 'Your offence was that you interfere with their operations. We have come to inform you that we are right behind you, protecting you so that you can continue your good works.'

Enitan looked puzzled. He hesitated for a while, thinking of how to get more information from him. He asked, 'why do you want to protect me from them? If I need protection from anyone, surely it's not from you. I'll simply file a report against them.'

Storm smiled. This guy was playing with fire and dicing with his life, he thought with amusement. 'Let me ask you how many times have students called on the government to fight the war on campus and how many times they have succeeded.'

Enitan again looked hesitant. It was true that the government had not been able to help the students. Each time there was a conflict among the cults, the police often found it hard to know who was fighting what. At the end of the day, the school would be asked to close for a while. When the students resumed, there would be peace for a while before something - anything triggered another conflict.

'You know the government cannot help us,' Storm said. 'That is the reason we have the Red Eyes on campus. You can call us whatever you like - bad guys, secret cults or whatever but you must realize that we are vigilante. You know very well that sometimes it takes a criminal to catch a criminal. Sometimes you find some elements of criminal act in the activities governments of all nations. The so-called secret service is more or less a criminal set up. What makes them not to look like criminals is the fact that they are established by the law. In America for instance, there are some police that are called undercover policemen. They get involved in crimes just because they want to get proofs to convict a criminal. Even then, those ones are diplomatic. There are some agents even right here in Nigeria that get involved in crimes.'

'Are you trying to justify the killings which your cult is involved in?'

Storm waved impatiently. 'It seems difficult to convince fellowship guys like you that there are times we have to fight evil with evil, crimes with crimes, killings with counter killings. You can't fight all kinds of evils with good, can you? Even God have to massacre many people just to protect his own people - the Israelites. A good example is the story about the red sea.'

'You can dwell more on the New Testament of the Bible,' Enitan said, trying to take the opportunity to preach against violence which his cult was always involved in. He believed his vigilante group is fighting for justice but Jesus preached against killing one another. "God said it even in his law in the Old Testament that no one should kill.'

'But God kills.'

'Yes. He's the only one who has the right to take lives because he is God and he created all.'

'How about David whose hands, according to God were so filled with blood that he could not build the house of the Lord?'

Enitan was a little surprised that a cult member knew so much about the Bible. He asked involuntarily, 'are you a Christian?'

'You're leading me off the subject, my President,' Storm told him. 'We'll reserve that part of the discussion for another time.'

'Okay.'

'Now, this is for the record. You're the President of the Students' Union on this campus. We - I mean the Red Eyes ensured that you were elected the President.'

Enitan gave him a long stare. 'I'm hearing this for the first time.'

'Really? You think the Christians put you in that position?' Storm asked as if he was surprised at his sheer ignorance.

'God did, not you or anyone,' Enitan said even though he knew he would fault the argument.

'God did not come down from the sky nor sent his angels to put you on the throne, did he?' He asked and added after a brief pause, 'he uses people like us to get things done. Anyway, I've not come to tell you the game of campus politics but to tell you why The Black Skulls cannot stand your sight.'

Enitan looked at him with keen interest.

Storm stood up to pace in front of him. He said, 'there's more to what is happening than what you fellowship guys see. During the election into the post of the S. U. G President, your rival, Deyi, was selected by The Black Skulls as their candidate. We later got to know that he is their secret member. If the guy becomes the President, we'll be done for unless we morgue him. If we morgue him, there'll be war. We are peace loving guys.'

Enitan laughed for the first time.

Storm frowned at him. 'What's so funny?'

Still laughing, he replied, 'you make The Red Eyes sounds like a fine group.'

'We are fine group of people because we fight for justice and good courses.'

'The justice includes taking law into your hands. You and I know that there's nothing good about cultism.'

'We are not cultists. I keep telling you this.' He looked impatient, going to sit down again. 'We are vigilante group.'

'I'll like to know the difference between your vigilante group and secret cults,' Enitan said.

'There difference is in their objectives and purposes. You know sometimes you have to make war while pursuing good causes. The picture is like a country that needs soldiers to protect her. We're secret soldiers that protect the students against violent guys like The Black Skulls.'

'Let's not argue over that. You can continue with your story about making me the S. U. G President.'

Storm looked thoughtful for a while before he continued, 'when we heard that the Campus Christian Fellowship was presenting you as a candidate, we decided to throw our weight behind you. We know that you fellowship guys are quite harmless and predicable. Of course, that did not go well with The Black Skulls. We know they would look for opportunities to register their fury. So ever since then we've been keeping an eye on you. We don't want you to regret your position.'

'Even if I believe your story, you really expect me not to regret the position that exposes me to terrorists?'

'Sorry for that but the truth is: the price of good leadership is what you're paying for. Furthermore, you must understand that if good guys like you shy away from leadership positions, bad guys will find their way there. The good people would be the ones that would suffer most while the bad ones will flourish. That is the reason you must remain firm even in the face of threats.'

Enitan frowned with confusion.

Storm smiled at him, patting him on the shoulder and stood up again. 'That's food for your big heart, good head and sound mind.'

He waved at the other men to follow him, walking away.

Enitan began to feel uneasy after the conversation with Storm. So many things were going on in his mind. He now seemed to appreciate what people meant when they said politic is a dirty game. As the politics in campus was made dirty by some dirty students, so it was made dirty at the national level by unscrupulous elements of the society. Still good people must be involved in it otherwise, as Storm Redhead told him, the good people would be the ones to suffer.

He went to see Jide at his residence in the evening. After a brief exchange of pleasantries, he told him of his encounter with Storm, the leader of the Red Eyes. As Jide shared with him some snacks and drinks which he bought while coming from the lecture room, he narrated virtually everything Storm told him.

Jide patted him on the shoulder, smiling at him. 'Come on; let's take some snacks and drinks.'

'I'm not really excited now.'

'I know, brother,' Jide said, closing his eyes and spreading his hands over the snacks to bless the food. He smiled again at him. 'Let's eat now.' He took a bite out of his share, taking a gulp out of the drink directly from the pack.

Enitan could see he was really hungry. He began to take his slowly. 'I can smell conflict under my nose,' he said.

'Don't be bordered, my precious brother.'

Enitan looked at him as if to ask him if he did not care about what was about to happen.

'We cannot leave you alone to face the battle of this magnitude,' Jide told him, smiling. 'This is the moment we have to start the battle in the Spirit and pull down the strongholds of the devil. God have not created what he cannot control. So we're using power of the Lord to get victory even before the battle begins.' He paused for a while, taking another bite on the pie. 'I've raised a team of prayer warriors for you. I'm the leader of the team. We are bringing God into the battle. That's what matters, isn't it?'

Enitan nodded. He was glad that his people never left him on his own.

'While praying, there was a prophecy that we should fast for three days for no one but you. Today is the last day. You know one thing about leadership,' Jide continued as he ate the pie, washing it down with the drink. 'Leadership is not about one thing or one person. It's about many things and many people. Once it has involved all those things, you need God at the centre of everything. I studied the leadership of many people in the Bible and also in our generations. I noticed that their success depends on how close they are to God. You see, the people have a way of destroying your relationship with God with their demands, pressure and ideas. That's why it's good for leaders to move away from the crowd to be with God and hear clearly from him. There you can receive fresh anointing and inspiration to lead. Then there is this area of being firm. Many leaders compromise. That alone can destroy many things. The ability to make sound decision is one thing. To stand by it is quite another thing. It's so unfortunate that the set of people you're dealing with are different from the ones I'm leading. It's easy for you to compromise because you have to tolerate all kinds of people, including those who have made up their minds to serve the devil or their bellies. Once you realize this, you will know you have to take few godly people as your counsellors. I appreciate your humility - a wonderful quality of a leader. You always

85

come to me so that we can look at things together. As the word of God says, iron sharpens iron just as we are here to encourage each other. I use to tell people that one man cannot make heaven on his own. Someone has to lead him to Christ. Someone has to feed him with the word of God until his capable of leading others to Christ. The same thing goes for leadership. Every leader needs advisers and counsellors.'

'Yes,' Enitan who had been attentive said, nodding in complete agreement. 'There are many things you have influenced me to do. The funny thing is that when I successfully carried them out with the help of God, you don't get the credit.'

'I'm also a leader, remember,' Jide told him. 'So I know that a good leader is never interested in credits. All that matter is good result. What if you don't get good result, who get the blames? You, of course.'

Enitan smiled and said, 'yeah.'

'Well,' Jide said after a brief silence, still taking the snacks and drinks. 'As for your meeting with the Red Eyes leader, there's nothing to fear or to be bordered about. God tells us in his word that we should be still and know that he is the Lord. We don't know how he is going to fight the battle and it's not our duty to know. If he tells us how, fine. If he doesn't, why should we care how? All he has assured us in his word is that victory will be ours at end of it all. Remember we are more than conquerors through Christ who strengthens us.'

'Don't you think I should inform the school authority or the police?'

'You can only inform the University authority if at all you're to tell anyone,' Jide replied. 'But you must not tell anyone unless God specifically says you should. We have the privilege of getting directives from God. If we do things God does not tell us to do, we only make things complicated or get into serious trouble. The principle is: no directives, nothing to execute. Besides that, I am yet to be convinced that the school authority or even the police do not know anything about this.'

'Redhead, the leader of the Red Eyes told me it's no use telling anyone,' Enitan told Jide.

'That's true. The one we can report the matter to is God. He created everything in this world and there is nothing beyond his control.'

Enitan spent close to two hours with Jide before he decided to leave. Jide lead him in prayers before he left.

CHAPTER TEN

Storm was holding meetings with warriors of the Red Eyes at night, deliberating on their next move. They already discovered that the Black skulls were planning to strike the S. U. G President. Storm already dispatched some of the finest warriors of the Red Eyes to guard him at his residence.

Capo of The Black skulls who had been watching Enitan all along through their top secret members saw his chance to strike the Red Eyes when Storm met with the S. U. G President. He knew he must have gone to tell Enitan about the cold war between the two cults. Since Enitan had been informed of what was happening and since he has held meetings with both Storm and Capo at different times with different results, The Black Skulls could now assume that the S. U. G President was a secret member of the Red Eyes who was using him to thwart their operations on campus.

Capo had declared to all the members of the Black skulls that the S. U. G President was their enemy during a meeting with them. Of course, this made most of them, especially Moduola very eager to go into battle with the Red Eyes. 'It is hard to believe that the S. U. G President is a top secret member of the Red Eyes,' Capo told the rest even though he knew that was not true. 'I have proof and enough information that confirmed this. First, the Red Eyes did all they could to get Enitan into the position of the S. U. G President so that they can make use of him to make offensive move against us. Since he became the president, he's been stepping on our toes deliberately. The last straw that broke the camel's back was the case of the guy called Richard. Richard offended us and I made a deal with him and decided that if he could defeat one of us in a fight, we'll let him go. If he was not able to defeat him, we'll get him initiated. You were here. Slippery Demon was the one that fought and defeated him. We were supposed to initiate him with the other guys the following day but the S. U. G President, knowing fully well that he had the Red Eyes as his warriors, had the audacity to tell Richard to leave the campus. As if that was not insulting enough, he had the guts to come to me and informed me that he is S. U. G president who has what it takes to crush us. He said our group in being funded by unscrupulous people in the society. In short, he declared war against the Black skulls through all sorts of things he said.

'I have to tell you all these so that you can see the reason we have to go into war against the Red Eyes. The war is not a way to boast my or our egos but a way to defend our dignity and pride. If the S. U. G President and his useless protectors go away with all the insults we've received from them so far, we'll all lose our faces as members of The Black skulls. As you all know, maintaining the dreadful name of The Black skulls is what gives us strengths and relevance even among our godfathers and clients. If the name goes down the drain, mark my words, we'll all go down with it.

'At this point, I want to ask all of you: who wants to belong to a group that has lost her face? No one! So let's give our enemies a bit of what we are - bloodshed!'

When Storm got the information that The Black skulls were planning to strike the S. U. G President, he dispatched some Red Eyes tough soldiers to protect him wherever he went and at his resident. He wished he could get detailed information about the plans of The Black skull but his sources did not have access to the details. In other not to take chances he told those guarding the S. U. G President to call him immediately if they suspected that the Black Skulls are mobbing around him. He also ensured that all warriors of the Red Eyes were to be at standby and ready for war at the slightest notice.

By now, of course, the S. U. G President had become the central focus of the two giant cults on campus. Though he suspected The Red Eyes were always around, he never knew The Black skulls were much more around. They were all waiting for the Capo to tell them when to strike. As Capo planned it, he wanted to create the impression that S. U. G President was "slaughtered" during a conflict between two cults without indicating in anyway that he was actually their target. So he told them they should inform him of all his movements.

Somehow Enitan has built the courage and faith that made him believe that, no matter what happened, God would protect him. So he did not border much about what seemed to be coming his way. Jide and some leaders of other Christian Fellowships who had been informed to pray for the safety of the S. U. G President and other students were always around to embolden him. One of them in the music department even gave him one of the songs he was inspired by God to write specifically for him.

What am I supposed to do
When I am weighed down?

As for me, I will think of Jesus
When I am confused about my life
Jesus has the plan of my life
I can trust him to be in charge

What am I supposed to do…?

When the battle is getting tough
I think of how Jesus conquered death
When people persecute my life
I think of my home in heaven.

What am I supposed to do…?

When there is need for sacrifice
I always feel the joy to make it
Anytime I lose anything for Christ
I will always count my blessing

What am I supposed to do…?

When there is time to tell stories
I won't tell the stories of woes
I will share my testimonies
Of how God gives me victories

What am I supposed to do…?

He was really encouraged by the song lyrics and how the entire Christian Fellowships rallied round him to fight the battles with him. To them, his victory belonged to them and his defeat was the defeat of the entire Christians on campus. So many of them have been praying and denying themselves of food for days. If there was anything he really enjoyed in all that was happening, it was the love of the Christians.

They were really wonderful people and he would readily lay down his life for any of them. This was the kind of love they learnt from Jesus who brought them together as a family.

The very night the Red eyes were holding a meeting was the time the Black skulls struck at Enitan's residence. The Capo of the Black Skulls had been duly informed of the number of the Red Eyes that were guarding the S. U. G President at his residence. He sent out the warriors that out numbered them.

Meanwhile, Storm was giving the rest of the Red eyes warrior the details of what the Black skulls were up to. 'They claimed that the S. U. G President interfered with their business whereas he has actually doing what is right. They tried to compel a guy called Richard to be one of them. Instead of joining them, he ran to S. U. G President who decided to talk with the Capo of the Black skulls to leave him alone. We know who the Black skulls are. Once they mark someone as their member, they would do all they could to initiate him. The Capo felt that the S. U. G President declared war against the Black skulls when he tried to help the guy. Actually, they have been looking for ways to strike him since he was elected President. They feel this is their chance.

'I met with the President this afternoon. He gave me the impression that he is not comfortable with his position as the President,' Storm told members of the Red Eyes. There were a very good number of them, having a meeting that night. 'If we allow anything to happen to him, he'll have every reason to resign from the position and any evil minded individual will then have an easy ride to this post.'

'That would be a defeat on our own part if that happens,' one of them said. Storm smiled at him. 'You're right. Besides that, we don't know of any other good guy who would be courageous enough to challenge the insanity of these evil ones on campus. This is a President that is after the promotion of peace on this campus. But the Black Skulls are looking for war. We all know that they'll not make war with those who are ready to fight them but they'll fight the innocent and the defenseless victims. It's time we let them know what we stand for. Therefore, we shall make war with The Black Skulls if they try to hurt the S. U. G President. Those who are not here are already on standby. We don't know when Black Skulls will strike but we are ready for them anytime. As I speak, seven men are camping round the President's residence. From the information I have, I don't expect the Capo of the Black Skulls to send more than three guys down there since he feels he's an easy target....' His mobile phone interrupted him, ringing in his pocket. He quickly picked it after looking at the screen briefly. 'Ya? Scorpion. Talk to me... What?' He listened with rapt attention. After a while, he said, 'go and get the President out of his room and tell the boys to keep them busy. We'll be right there with back you up.' He hurriedly put the phone back into his pocket. He said in a flat voice, 'the boys had been outnumbered. The Black Skulls are striking at the President's residence. Guys! This is the time for action... Let's get our weapons and go now!'

As the rest moved to their weapons, he began to make series of phone calls to other members of the Red Eyes who were at standby.

*   *   *   *   *

Enitan was sleeping when the forces of the Red Eyes and the Black Skulls gathered for war right outside his residence. When the shooting began, he woke up with a start and hurried to peep through the window of his room that was in semi-darkness. For the first in his entire life, he witnessed real war right in the school where leaders was supposed to be bred. The killings of members of both cults horrified him. Was this a horror movie or a nightmare or a reality? He began to shiver, not with fear but with the horror of people killing one another because of him. What must he do? Should he go to them and offer himself just to stop the killings? Just as he was contemplating whether to go out or not, two stout, tough looking men burst the door open. Each of them held a gun.

Enitan did not know who they were. He held his hands up slowly and said with passion. 'It's me you want. Take me and stop the killings.'

Don, as one of them was simply called said, 'we can't stop them, S.U G President.'

When he called him S. U. G President, he knew they were Red Eyes. He put down his hands.

'We've come to rescue you. You're under serious attack and we have been outnumbered. You have to come with us to a save place. We can't protect you here but we'll soon get a back up that would handle the warriors of the Black skulls.'

Enitan looked hesitant. The other man called Slage roughly took his hand and led him towards the door. He first peeped through

91

the door. Two Black Skulls were facing their direction with their guns.

'Lie down,' Slage told the other two men. They lay on their bellies and began to craw out of the room slowly and gently with Slage taking the lead, Enitan in the middle and Don at the rear. They crawled out of sight or so it seemed but Capo has all his focus on the house where the three men were coming out from.

He smiled to himself, gestured on the men to engage the Red Eyes while he and Moduola went after the three men. Each of the two men held an automatic gun.

By now there were wails, shouting and screams of horror among the student residents in the area. Most of them have fled their rooms to find places to hide. A few of them were wounded but only members of both the Red Eyes and the Black skull were dying as the conflicts began to reach its peak. More and more Red Eyes trooped in from various directions.

The Red Eyes were either helping some residents to escape from the area or shooting at members of the Black skulls whom they were able to identify through the logo of the Black skulls on bands that were tied round their left arms or head.

When the Red Eyes seemed to be gaining upper hand, Storm looked round for the S. U. G president. When he could not find him, he called Scorpion on the phone. He told him he had to send Don and Slage to rescue the President while he commanded the warriors. Storm called Don at once. He was told of their location. He went towards the place at once.

Enitan had no idea where he was until Storm called Don. He said in frustration, 'I wish I know what is going on. Why do people have to kill others?"

Don snorted, 'I don't think you need any explanation before you know what exactly is happening. This is just a proof of the reality of the story you were told.'

'Why are they doing this?' Enitan could not help asking. 'I'm going to report them.'

Slage snorted, 'you don't need to border about that for now. Think of your safety first. Dead people tell no tales, man. Besides, there are more than enough dead bodies out there that can attract the attention of the police.'

Don slightly lifted his hand and stopped short when he heard the sound of footsteps behind them. 'Wait... I think there is someone around.' As he looked round, there is a gunshot. Slage went on his knees and fell on his face with a bullet wound on his back. Don shot at the direction but another gunshot went off.

Don and Enitan laid flat on the ground.

Enitan looked troubled as he lied still, beginning to pray. 'Lord, I pray that you forgive me all I have done wrong. Forgive also those who want me dead for they do not know what they are doing.'

The footsteps came closer. As Don and Enitan looked up, they see Capo with Moduola and Magol with guns, walking towards them.

Capol gave them a triumphant smile. 'That's supposed to be your last prayer, isn't it?'

Magol took Don's gun from him.

Enitan looked at Capo and asked in a whisper. 'Banjo… Why?'

'You and your so-called protectors provoked me,' Capo said in a snarl.

'And you preferred to waste lives because you've provoked? Come on....'

Capo walked round them briefly before he said, 'I warned you when you interfere in our business, didn't I? But you feels no qualms about it. You do realize then that you declared war against us with your provocative utterances. I warned you to stay clear of this but, instead of heeding my warning, you boasted about your position as the S. U. G President. You were so sure of yourself that you underrated who we are.'

'But you know I don't mean it this way. I meant to make peace with you... I'm sorry if I offend you.'

Capo laughed. 'That's too late now, boy.'

'Come on, please, stop the bloodshed....'

'Now, now, don't give me the impression that you're such a weak leader. I thought you're strong!'

Don out of infuriation snorted, 'leave him alone, man! He's not your target. We all know that.'

'On the contrary,' Capo said, glaring at him, 'he's been our main target. We've been looking for the opportunity to hit him since he became the S. U. G President. We know you guys put him in the position so that you can use him.'

'That's not true!' Enitan said.

'What if it's true?' Don groaned.

Moduola snarled, 'silence, you fool...' He kicked Don on the wounded shoulder.

'If what makes leaders strong is the bloodshed of those they are supposed to protect, I'll rather be a weak leader,' Entan said.

Capo roared with laughter and then pulled Enitan on his feet.

'You're admitting that you're a weak leader now?'

'Don't fool yourself,' Don said. 'He's not. At least he is able to stand up against your mad group and all your madness.'

'I say silence, you block head!' Moduola roared at him, kicking him again.

'Yes, I am a weak leader,' Enitan said. 'Please, Banjo, don't kill us.'

Capo laughed, enjoying himself. 'Go on your knees!'

Enitan knelt down. 'I would have loved to spare your life so that I can order you around but you've seen too much.'

'Please, Banjo...' Enitan pleaded again. 'Haven't you seen enough blood, flowing everywhere on campus - the blood of the future leaders of Nigeria? God doesn't like this.'

'Well, let your God save you if you so believe in him,' Capo said in amusement.

'We are not bordered about our lives.' Don told him.

'Yes, we're not so bordered about this life,' Enitan agreed.

Capo pointed his gun at him. 'Now you're talking like a brave leader. Do you want to die first, my guy?'

Enitan closed his eyes, expecting the bullet to go off.

Suddenly there were three gun concurrent shots. Capo and the other two men fell down with loud thuds. They are covered with blood.

Enitan opened his eyes, surprised that he was still alive, still unhurt but the sight of Capo and his men that were covered with their own blood horrified him. He frantically looked round while Don went to take his gun.

Suddenly Storm and other Red Eyes guys went closer to them as if they were dropped from the sky.

Enitan concluded that this must be a miracle. God is always on time.

Storm smiled at Enitan, gave him his hand. He took it and stood up slowly. 'You're save now, S. U. G President. It's never too late for your God to send helper too you, is it?'

Enitan was yet to find his tongue. He was too confused to say anything.

While the other Red Eyes guys went to attend to Slage who was still alive though unconscious as a result of loss of much blood, Don went to the Capo and his men who were dying or pretending to have died. He began to shoot each of them on the head, starting with Capo.

'Stop it!' Enitan cried at him.

'You're a crazy guy,' Don told him.

'This is wrong, you know. I'm not part of it,' Enitan said.

Storm looked at Don. 'He's a Christian. He had been programmed to tamper justice with mercy.' He looked at Enitan. 'These guys are ruthless. They'll come after you again if we don't get rid of them now. They are the remaining top guys in The Black Skulls that need to be wiped out.'

'No,' Enitan insisted. 'Being ruthless does not give you the right to kill them!'

'What do you suggest we do with them?' Storm asked. 'Spare them?'

'We'll hand them over to the police.'

'Do you have any idea how many lives were lost because of these guys?'

'No, I don't. But killing them does not justify…'

'What do you know about justice, my President?' Storm interrupted him, looking angry. 'Tell me!'

'I don't believe in extrajudicial killings,' he replied. 'Let the police handle the case.'

'They will get extrajudicial pardon from the police if they make one or two phone calls. I don't believe extrajudicial pardon is justice,' Storm retorted. 'Perhaps if these guys have shot you in the place that hurts you, you'll have a different opinion.' He looked at Don. 'Do your job, man.'

'No, please.'

'This is war, my President and I'm in charge here,' Storm declared.

Don fired the rest of the Black Skulls on the heads without further delay.

Storm grabbed Enitan's hand and led him out of the place. The rest of the Red Eyes followed him, carrying Slage who was still unconscious with them.

*　　*　　*　　*　　*

Titi watched the television with rapt attention while Richard and the rest were in their rooms. She was listening to the news about the bloodshed on campus. The news caster related the news about the conflict between two cults and how it was difficult to identify the cause.

95

Most students who were eye witnesses were either afraid to give details of what actually happened or not sure of what actually happened. However, many of them confirmed that there were more dead students than the number of corpses found. This invariably gave the media the impression that there were many missing corpses. Although many innocent students were wounded, there were proofs that most of the dead students were either members of the secret cult called the Black skulls or the other cults which could not be identified.

'Richard!' Titi called on him after she realized that the bloodshed took place in his school.

'Yes, mum,' he answered, coming out of the room to join her in the sitting room.

She pointed at the television and said, 'did you hear what happened in your school?'

'Yes,' he said indifferently and went to sit down opposite her.

'How did you know?'

'My friends in the school told me on the phone.'

'I'm sure this is what God revealed to the pastor in the dream,' she said.

'I guess so.' He apparently did not look happy.

'I wonder what is happening on campuses in this country,' she said as if she was talking to herself. Just then a knock sounded on the door. 'Please, come inside.'

The pastor, a prudent looking man entered the sitting room with a smile. 'Hello, everybody!'

'Pastor!' Titi said excitedly. She waved impatiently at the television. 'I just heard the news that there was bloodshed in Richard's school just as you dreamt it.'

'I see.' The pastor looked interested and glanced at the TV but the news was already over.

Richard who was standing up when he came in waved to a seat. 'You're welcome, sir. Please, have your seat.'

The Pastor smiled at him and patted him on the shoulder. 'Praise God, you didn't witness the bloodshed, did you?

'No, sir,' Richard answered silently. He was not himself ever since he was told that the S. U. G President nearly lost his life when he was caught up between the two cults that were fighting over him. He was almost sure that there would not be any bloodshed if he had allowed Jacob to influence him to be a devoted Christian. Even then, he wondered what would have happened if Jacob had not dragged the Christian Fellowship President who dragged the S. U. G president into the mess. He remembered that the S. U. G President tried to opt out, probably because he knew the implications of getting involved with the affairs of the secret cults. He almost lost his life in the cult conflict while trying to prevent the bloodshed. He, Richard who was cause of almost everything that happened was left out of the scene. Many people have died just because he did not take to a sound advice. He now appreciated what the Pastor meant when he said while preaching last Sunday that omission to do the right thing was unrighteousness. He even quoted a place in the Bible which he could not remember very well. The passage said something like "he who knows how to do good but refuses to do it, to him it is a sin."

The Pastor read it through the expression on his face that he was puzzled about something. He asked, 'what is wrong, Richard?'

He looked startled and said, 'em… it's nothing… I was just thinking of my friends among those who are dead?'

Titi asked impatiently, 'who are your friends among the dead secret cult members or those who are connected with them?'

'Oh, no mum,' he said quickly. 'My friends are those who are in the Christian Fellowship. The Student Union Government President is a member of the Christian Fellowship. I was told he almost lost his life while trying to bring peace into the campus.'

'You seem to have more information about what happened there,' the Pastor said. 'Can you tell us what actually happened in the school?'

Richard knew if he told them he was involved in the conflict and how close he was to be initiated into secret cult, his mother would have an heart attack. So he simply said, 'the only thing I know was that cults were fighting because one cult tried to compel a student to join while the other opposed it. We heard that the cults were planning to fight. So I came home. That's all I can say.'

'I see,' the pastor said with a sigh and looked at Titi. 'There's really nothing to worry about since God is control of all those who believe in him.'

'Pastor,' Titi said, unconsciously expressing her fear, 'don't you think it would be better if my son runs his program on part time.'

'Mum,' Richard said quickly, 'it's quite too late to do that now. Besides, part-time cost much more money and more years to run.'

'Madam,' Pastor said, 'like I said, there's nothing to worry about. Our lives are in save his hands - the hands of Jesus. If we try to play safe when we are in save hands, we only show our lack of confidence and trust in Christ. Lack of confidence in God is the real danger zone.

97

The safe zone is trust in God. I've seen so many people trying to play safe only to play into the hands of the devil or danger. Life itself is full of dangers and battles. As you know, there is no comfort zone in battles just as there is no save place in this world except in Jesus. Just trust in God and all will be well. I remember the song which the choir composed a few weeks ago. I love the song so much that I asked for the lyrics and even preached with it. It goes like this.

When you find your self in ocean of insanity
You need to keep you sanity if you want to survive
When the mountains threaten to swallow you at every side
You must look up to the Lord who is ready to save you.

Whenever there is battle for you to fight in this life.
Remember that the battle belongs to the Lord of host
If you are surrounded by the enemies anywhere
Jesus will see to it that no one touches his anointed

When you are tempted to take control of your life from God
Just because your world is up side down like a sleeping bat
Your life can be wrecked like a car that has an accident
Trust the Lord who has got the whole world in his hand.

After chatting and encouraging them, the pastor asked for the rest of the family and prayed with them.

*   *   *   *   *

It was about two weeks after the bloodshed on campus was over that everything seemed to come back to normal. So far now only the Black skulls were identified as the murderous cult that was responsible for the deaths of students who fought back in defense. With the deaths of most of their key members, including the Capo, the cult was crushed. If at all the group would rise up again, it would take a very long time.

The Red Eyes who lost twelve members with seven of them seriously wounded were regarded as heroes for saving many lives. The S. U. G executives felt obliged to cover them for saving the life of the President especially when they were implicated in the cause of the investigation. All the dead and wounded members of the Red Eyes, therefore, were regarded as the innocent students that became victims for trying to resist the Black skulls' their murderous activities.

The whole scenarios were so complicated that the more the police tried to investigate the cause of the bloodshed, the more different versions of the story they came up with. At last, it was concluded that some students who did not want to be compelled to join the secret cults ganged up to fight the Black skulls who planned to initiate the S. U. G President by force. When the President in question was asked to state his own version of the story, he simply told them that two students came into his rooms to rescue him from the Black skulls. He was taken to another place when the Capo and other members of the Black skulls ambushed him. They tried to kill the students that rescued him. As the Capo was about to shoot him dead, another set of students came to rescue him.

So many stories went round the campus but surprisingly the name of the Red Eyes was never mentioned. Even Richard who came into the school two weeks after he heard the news did not know about the Red Eyes. He only gathered that there was a vigilante group involved in the conflict.

Richard went to meet Jacob in his room, hoping to get details from him at his residence. He still felt sorrowful and responsible for the deaths of forty-six students, including the so-called innocent students.

'Hay, Richard!' Jacob said excitedly when he saw him. 'You came back at last!'

Richard went to sit down on his bed and said quietly, 'it's like a nightmare coming back to the campus when I heard about the bloodshed - the killings - all because of me.'

Jacob went to sit close to him. 'Oh, come on. You didn't cause it. So don't blame yourself. You're just a catalyst that sped up the occurrence of the inevitable on campus.'

'When I think of how the horror began, I could not help blaming myself for my inability to control my temper - for doing what I ought not to have done while what I ought to do suffers neglect.'

'Remember what would be would be. There's nothing you can do about that,' Jacob said, standing up to get his book. 'We still have every reason to thank God. With what has happened, the backbone of the Black Skulls is broken. It'll take them a long time to recover. By that time you will be long gone out of this college.'

'I heard that another cult is involved in the killings.'

'That is The Red Eyes but they were covered by the S. U. G.'

'Why?'

'Some say they are the secret service and the invisible army of the Students' Union Government. My brother, it's hard to explain or justify but I was told many of them died while saving the life of the S. U. G President.'

'So I was told,' Richard said. 'That makes me feel guilty the more.'

'I told you there is no need to feel bad about yourself. Perhaps you will feel better if I tell you that the Black Skulls had been looking for reason to attack the S. U. G President. They just used you as a way to get at him.'

'Why do they hate him that much?'

'It's a long scary story but I guess it's strictly because he uses his position to protect students from them.'

'I guess as much.'

'It was God that saved his life.'

Richard sighed and muttered, 'Lord of mercy.' He looked at Jacob and asked, 'is there any chance of getting rid of secret cults on campus?'

'I honestly don't know. I think what is important is that those who value their lives must not be part of them.'

*   *   *   *   *

Jide stands before the students at the Campus Fellowship hall to address the students that were gathered to hear the testimony about the saving grace of the Lord. Of course, some secret members of the Red Eyes were among them.

Jide said after sharing with the students how the Christians prayed for Enitan when there were threats of conflict, 'having given you the background of what led to the deaths of forty-six members of different secret cults, I would invite the S. U. G President, our precious brother Enitan to address us.'

The audience clapped as Enitan silently went to stand on the platform to address them.

'First of all, I'll like to appreciate God for sparing my life till now.' He was silent for a while, thinking that there was no use sharing his ugly experience with them. 'I was very close to death but God delivered me. God used other students who were ready to die just to protect me against the cultists. Some of them died, as you all know... Although there are so many things in my mind which I would love to express but because I don't have the time, I'll go straight to say few important things.' He paused again for a while before he continued, 'I

100

would have resigned my appointment as the S. U. G President after going through the recent trauma if not for what someone told me at the beginning of the crisis on this campus. He said that if good guys shy away from leadership positions, bad guys will find their ways to these posts but the good people would be the ones that would suffer the consequences. Besides that, Edmund Burke said that the only thing necessary for the triumph of evil is for good people to do nothing.'

He was silent as the students gave him another round of applause. He waved at them, smiling.

They stopped clapping before he continued.

'If I had not been a Christian, I would either be dead by now or leading the people astray. As Christians or good people, we must always campaign against cultism. Any evil oriented cultism, especially secret one is a menace to humanity. Our recent experience had shown that the activities of these evil one had cost the lives of so many people that are supposed to be blessings to our country, Nigeria. Cultism by its very nature does not only promote violence and killings but also kills the dreams of the nation. Most, if not all of us are sent here by our parents with the hope that we'll be trained as responsible human beings they'll be proud of. The moment a person joints secret cults, he shatters the dream of his family and the nation at large.' He began to pace round the platform. 'There is this tract that was published by the Campus Christian Fellowships. It is titled: Behold, Your Power Of Choice Can Destroy You. If you read the tract, you'll see that we all have the power of choice which is destructive if it is not handed over to Christ. This power is what makes us small gods. Angels in heaven don't have this power. In other words, the angels don't have any choice but to do what God tells them. God gives us the power to choose, making our lives to be full of choices. We have the power to choose between God and Satan, right and wrong, good and bad, light and darkness, positive and negative, righteousness and unrighteousness. The list is endless. This power is too dangerous for you and me to keep. People have used it to destroy themselves and others. It can destroy you if you don't hand it over to Jesus Christ.

'If all good people keep campaigning against all forms of evils everywhere, all the dry bones in our lives, families, communities, campuses, Nigeria and even the world at large will come back to life. Then we'll have cause to sing...'

Dry bones shall rise again...
Lord Jehovah is able to do all things

101

He's more than able
Dry bones shall rise up again…

    The rest of the students stood up and joined him in praising and singing to the Lord.

SUCCESSFUL CHRISTIANITY AND BASIC MINISTRIES

ISBN: 978-49874-6-0

A Collection Of Resource Materials That Precedes Christian Ministries And Basic Leadership Course Book

The first question is how Christianity is practiced even in a hostile environment. Next to that is the question about the potentials of Christians in spite of their apparent limitations. The other issues are connected to the successes, deliverance, callings, basic ministries of all Christians and evangelism. Various schools of thoughts have attempted these questions but many answers only portray Christianity as a form of religion instead of a way of life as specified by God. Some answers give room for compromise, hypocrisies, dogmas and denominational doctrines. The misconceptions about these areas of Christianity have brought about worldliness instead of righteousness and false achievements instead of fulfillment.

This book which contains six different subjects had been used to hold seminars at various levels, train ministers and Christian workers in Bible Schools and to equip the Church. It explains in simple terms the seemingly complex issues on practice of Christianity, Potentials, Deliverance, God's Kind Of Success, Evangelism and Basic Ministries of a Christian with Biblical principles, life transforming stories and illustrations.

CHRISTIAN MINISTRIES AND BASIC LEADERSHIP

ISBN: 978-36348-7-9 ISBN: 978-978-36348-7-9

A Collection Of Resource Materials That Follows Up Successful Christianity And Basic Ministries Course Book

As it is common to say that the hood does not make a monk, the dignified positions and bogus titles of many Christian leaders in modern days do not really make them Gospel Ministers.

This course book - a compilation of five resource materials on Missions And Outreach Ministries, Christian Communication Arts, Christian Leadership, Christian Education Methodology and Ministries Of Improvisations - aims at making every matured Christian an effective minister and leader at their respective homes, communities and nations. It teaches various ways Christians can communicate the word of God, meeting up to their responsibilities as ministers and leaders that reconcile people to God, edifying the Body Of Christ and reaching out to souls at the same time.

All of the resource materials are in use in Bible Schools like College Of Christian Education And Missions, in Churches and other ministries to raise Christian workers, Evangelists, Missionaries and other Ministers that serve at various levels and leadership capacities.

INSANITY OF HUMANITY

ISBN: 978-36348-6-0 ISBN: 978-978-36348-6-2

The Results Of Research Works Into Various Methods Of Brainwashing

Man is made to exercise his freewill. The mind of his own and the power to choose between right and wrong, good and evil, light and darkness is about to be washed away through brainwashing. The agents of control dubbed as Secret Government by John Todd (the top Illuninati defector) have put necessary machinery in place to ensure that all human beings are in conformity in their thinking and ways of life, trying to wipe away diversity, which makes each person unique.

This book attempts to shed light on how the techniques of mind control are applied through the use of propaganda, education, entertainments, drugs, religions, media and other means of communications. It is the result of research works, some of which are based on findings of various researchers and writers like Bugger Lugz, Edward Hunter, Hadley Cantril, Herbert Krugman, David L. Robb, Vaughan Bell, Juliana Gomez, Ryan Duffy Vice, Henry Makow, David Nicholls, Fritz Springmeire, Steven Hassan, Renate Thienel, Debra Pursell, Mary Pride and a host of others who are acknowledged in this book.

THE UNROMANTIC LOVE BIRDS

ISBN: 978-4987-5-7 ISBN: 978-978-4974-5-5

And other short stories about love and marriages

They were very much in love right from their school days but when they got married and had children, romance became the game Charles' wife refused to play. No matter how much he tried to make her understand the unbearable condition her unromantic attitude has subjected him into, she would not change. Consequently, after enduring for so long, he was forced to look for the women that would make up for her weakness. He unofficially married a beautiful lady of insane jealousy. Though she was ready to give him what was missing in his marriage, it soon dawn on him that he has solved one big problem only to create a bigger one.

THE BATTLE OF THE CONQUERORS

ISBN: 978-49874-7-3 ISBN: ISBN: 978-978-49874-0-7-9

Wickedness takes over the land of Bondage from First Couple and subjects everybody into slavery without giving anybody the chance to be free. Love brings The Redeemer from Eternity and offers the slaves the chance to escape. Wickedness soon declares war and engages everyone in the battle. The Redeemer makes the redeemed people Conquerors by giving them the armour of war and Comforter but Wickedness cannot be undone. He has several thousands of years of experience in the war. So he is quick to recognize the weakness of the redeemed people who are ignorant of their strengths and advantages. Although the Conquerors fight like immutable giants, rescuing victims of war, many people suffer heavy casualties.

Since King Wickedness knows that a redeemed person is strong enough to chase one thousand of his warriors at a time, and two would put ten thousand into flight, he enlists as one of his warriors the people's deadliest enemy called Disunity.

Wickedness is able to strike the people by making them to fight with one another, turning what is supposed to be their best moments in the battle into tales of woes.

NETWORK BIBLE CLUB
YOUTH AND ADULT BOOK ONE
ISBN: 978 - 978- 49874-9-X ISBN: 978-978-49874-9-3
A collection of 26 life transforming stories, 26 poems, 26 hymn tuned songs and weekly Bible lessons

The issue of moral instructions in schools and at homes is threatened with extinction. Consequently, so many youths are involved in prostitution, drug addictions, cultism, fraudulent practices, armed robberies and other crimes. Those who are supposed to be trained as leaders in various walks of life are the ones posing serious threats to many lives. Many parents who fail to add moral values to the upbringing of their children often times breed potential criminals under their roofs without knowing it. Apart from these, many other people negatively influence young ones through the media, music, publications, films, conduct and foul language; making them to lose their moral and family values.

This book one just like the rest of other volumes is an attempt to bring back moral instructions into schools and campuses through the use of stories, hymn tuned songs, poems, Bible lessons and class activities. It is designed to assist teachers and ministers in Secondary Schools, Bible Clubs, Churches and Campus Fellowships to teach people, especially youths the Word of God and serves as a school text book in subjects relating to literature, music and other creative works.

FOUNDATION BIBLE CLUB A-Z STORY BOOK
ISBN: 978-49874-2-2 ISBN: 978-978-49874-2-4
Volume 1 With 26 Stories, 26 Bible
Lessons, 26 Rhymes And 26 Songs For Book For Young Minds

An adage says, "a man who builds a house without building his child builds what the child will later sell." Proverbs 22:6 says, "train up a child in the way he should go: and when he is old, he will not depart from it." This book is an attempt to assist parents and teachers to meet up to the challenges that befall them in carrying out this important function in the light of the moral decadence that is prevailing all over the world.

The first edition of the book was used by several thousands of teachers, ministers and parents in schools, Churches and homes to build the moral values of young ones. Apart from the stories, songs and Bible passages for the young ones to study, there is a seminar material that is based on the lecture which the author delivered to school proprietors, children ministers and Christian professionals in this volume.

RANSOM FOR LOVE
ISBN: 978-49874-8-1 ISBN: 978-978-4987-4-8-6

She accepted his marriage proposal without knowing the kind of person he was. She soon discovered that he was a mean and ruthless guy who was always ready to get whatever he wanted by all means even if he has to pay for it with the lives of others. She was in his bondage, especially when her parents who believed he was a generous and gentleman were on his side.

Because she considered the proposal to marry him as a marriage engagement with the devil incarnate, she decided that she would rather die than to share her life with him. Then out of the blues, this passionate gentleman sneaked into her life despite all she did to discourage him. She could not resist his love for her when he offered to set her free from the devil incarnate. Then the battle began – sooner than they anticipated.

THE WEIGHT OF DEATH

ISBN: 9978-36348-0-1 ISBN: 978-978-36348-0-0

(Story Of The Spirit Eyes Series)

PLAY ONE: HORROR IN THE FAMILY: Talimi probably did not envisage his death when he was trying to compel his son, Damola to succeed him in the occult Brotherhood. Other members of the secret cult were aware of the battle between them. So when Talimi died; his family, especially Damola who was a diehard Christian began to fall prey to the cult. Using all their powers and the spirit that posed as Talimi's ghost, the cult waged war against the family, tormenting and making them to be at loggerheads.

PLAY TWO: RITUAL KIDS' KIDNAPPERS: Victor and the rest of the members of the School Bible Club were taught that there are lots of evil people in this world but he did not understand why God allowed him to be among the children that were taken away from their parents. He soon understood that he was to be used by God to rescue other children who did not know that everyone that truly believes in Jesus has the power to overcome evil.

PLAY THREE: THE WEIGHT OF DEATH: Awoseun would not have known the real source of problems of mankind if his father had not given him the power to see demons tormenting the people in different ways. What he was yet to know, however, was the power of light over darkness. When he was caught in crossfire between these powers, he desperately sought for deliverance.

CALVARY ROCK RESOURCE BOOKLETS

ISSN: 1595 93X

The Quarterly Missionary Booklets That Are Designed To Teach Children, Youths And Adults In Schools, Fellowships, Churches, At Homes, Office And Other Places.

Although all the various volumes of this booklet can be used independently of other books but it is recommended that it should be used as part of supplementary materials to make up for Foundation and Network Bible Club Story Books for both children and adults in School, Church, Campus, Office and other Fellowships.

Each of the volume is rich with quarterly Bible lessons, stories, drama, songs, seminar, tract materials and a host of other things that can be used to edify, educate, entertains and evangelize every category of people, ranging from children to elderly persons.

Every volume is designed to equip school teachers, ministers in Churches or campus or office fellowships and other people who wish to work with the Lord.

All These And Other Books Are Distributed Worldwide And Published By The Publishing House Of Calvary Rock Resources

*Ikenne-Remo, Nigeria
*Manchester, United Kingdom
*New York, United States

www.calvaryrock.org

www.ingramcontent.com/pod-product-compliance
Lightning Source LLC
Chambersburg PA
CBHW031846170626
46807CB00004B/1645